Shopping for a Billionaire 1

by Julia Kent

When mystery shopper Shannon Jacoby meets billionaire Declan McCormick with her hand down a toilet in the men's room of one of his stores, it's love at first flush in this hilarious new romantic comedy from *New York Times* bestselling author Julia Kent.

Copyright © 2014 by Julia Kent

Sign up for my New Releases and Sales email list at my blog to get the latest scoop on new eBooks, freebies and more:

http://jkentauthor.blogspot.com/p/sign-up-for-my-new-releases-email-list.html

Table of Contents

Chapter One

I am eating my ninth cinnamon raisin bagel with maple horseradish cream cheese and hazelnut chocolate spread.

Don't judge me.

It's my job to eat this.

It's a Monday morning, 9:13 a.m. on the dot, and the counter person, Mark J., takes exactly seventeen seconds to acknowledge my presence. He then offers to upsell my small mocha latte, which I decline nicely, and within seventy-three seconds my cinnamon raisin bagel with maple horseradish cream cheese and hazelnut chocolate spread is in my hands, toasted and warm.

I pay my $10.22 with a $20 bill and he counts back my change properly, hands me a receipt and points out the survey I can complete for a chance to win a $100 gift card to this chain restaurant.

Survey? Buddy, I'm surveying you *right now*.

No, I don't have obsessive-compulsive disorder, though it helps in my line of work. I am not a private detective, and I don't have an unhealthy stalker thing for Mark J., who loses points for ringing up a customer, touching cash, and not washing his hands before touching the next person's bagel.

I cringe at mine.

I'm a secret shopper. Mystery shopper. Or as the clerks and managers in the stores where I pretend to be a regular shopper call me: Evil Personified.

That's *Ms.* Evil Personified to you, buddy.

It really *is* my job to sit here on a sunny Monday morning, in my ninth chain store, buying the same exact meal over and over again, sipping each mocha latte and sliding a thermometer in the hot liquid to make certain the temperature is between 170 and 180 degrees Fahrenheit.

You try doing that without making people think you are that one weird customer, the one who talks to aliens through the metal shake cans, or who brings her teacup chihuahua in to share a grilled cheese and lets the dog lick the plate clean.

I'm just as weird, except I'm getting *paid* to do it.

My best friend and coworker, Amanda, created a little thermometer that looks just like a coffee stirrer. I slip it in through the lid and in sixty seconds—voila!

One hundred seventy-four degrees. I reach for my phone and pretend to send a text. I'm really opening my shopper's evaluation app, to type in all the answers to the 128 questions that must be properly answered.

I enter my name (Shannon Jacoby), today's date, the store location, whether the front trashcan was clean (it was), whether the front mats were clean (they were), the name of the clerk who waited on me (Mark J.), and pretty much every question you could imagine short of my favorite sexual position (none of your business) and the first date of my last period (who cares? It's not like I could possibly be pregnant. Maybe the cobwebs are in the way…).

Did I mention this is my ninth store of the day? I started at 5:30 a.m. I'm very, very questioned and cinnamoned *out*. One hundred twenty-eight questions times nine stores equals a big old identity crisis and a mouth that can't tell the difference between horseradish and mocha.

This is not my fault. I am in management for a secret shopper company. That means my job is to find people to do what *I'm* doing. A year ago, when I was a fresh-faced marketing major with my newly minted degree from UMass and $50,000 in student loans at the ripe old age of twenty-three, the job seemed like a dream.

You know those ads you see online to "Get Paid to Shop!"?

Yep. They're real. You really can sign on as a mystery shopper with various marketing companies, and once you pass some basic tests, you apply for jobs. What I'm doing right now pays your $10.22 expense, gives you the free breakfast sandwich and latte, and you earn a whopping $8 in payment about a month after submitting your mystery shopper report to our office.

And people are *lining up* to do this.

Except…sometimes, supervisors can't find

anyone to fill a last-minute no-show. I'm a full-time, salaried employee (which means I get to keep the sandwich, but not the $8 for each of these nine shops this fine, beautiful, bloated morning).

One of our flakier shoppers, Meghan, texted me at 4:12 a.m. to tell me the purple and green unicorn in her flying sparkly Hummer told her not to eat bagels anymore, and she couldn't make her nine—NINE!—breakfast shops on religious grounds.

Okay, then. Someone was eating something other than cinnamon raisin bagels last night, and I suspect it involved mushrooms of some sort.

That gave me one hour and eighteen minutes to find a replacement, which meant—yep—here I was. In a rush, I'd jumped out of bed, printed out all of Meghan's shops, made a driving plan and a map, and steadied myself for the biggest mystery-shopping blitz I'd done since—

Since being dumped by my ex-boyfriend last year. Steven Michael Raleigh decided that finishing his MBA meant he needed a trophy wife who could schmooze with all the hoity-toities on the Back Bay in Boston.

Me? A Mendon girl with only a BA who works as a "glorified fast food snitch" just didn't cut it, so he cut me loose.

So here I sit in this little coffee shop in West Newton, counting down the minutes until I can break into the men's room. That's right – the *men's* room. Did I mention I'm a DD cup? *So* not a covert Men's Room Ninja.

M y *ninth* men's room of the morning. Every part of the store has to be evaluated, including the toilets. You've seen one urinal, you've seen them all…except that's not how it works when you're evaluating a store for a mystery shop.

Nineteen questions about cleanliness and customer service are waiting for my answers. Neatly waiting inside my smartphone's app.

And if I didn't break in to the men's room?

The eval would be a "failed job." I shudder. A failed job is worse than eating nine cinnamon raisin maple horseradish bagels, because when you work in my field, a failed job is like a failed date with a billionaire.

Whatever went wrong, it's always, *always* your fault.

Speaking of billionaires, *hellllooooo*, Christian Grey. In walks a man wearing a suit that must cost more than my rickety old Saturn sedan. Fine grayish-blue with fibers that look like he snaps his fingers and they conform to his body because he's *that* dominant. Trim body with a flat, tapered torso, and *oh!* His jacket is unbuttoned. The bright white shirt underneath is so bespoke that it fits like a glove.

If I had echolocation I could map out the terrain of ab muscles through sheer force of will. His cut body is meant to be relief mapped the way Braille is meant to be read.

With my fingertips.

Parts of my body that have been in suspended animation since I dated Steve spring to life. Some of these parts, as I watch him reach out and shake hands with Mark J. and see the taut lines of sinew at his wrist, the sprinkle of sandy hair around a gold watch, haven't risen from the dead since my party days at UMass.

And then he opens his mouth and asks Mark J., "How's your morning going?"

Liquid smoke, whiskey, sunshine and musk pours out of that jaunty, sultry mouth and all over my body like I am standing under a waterfall of *oh, yeahhhhh*. Everything goes into slow motion around me. My world narrows to what I see, and I can't stop staring at Mr. Sex in a Suit.

Mark J. says something to the man in what sounds like Klingon, and they share a laugh. Beautiful, straight white teeth and cheeks that dimple—*dimple!*—make me fall even more in lust with Mr. I Will Make You Omelets in the Morning Wearing Your Suit Jacket and Nothing Else.

I look down and nearly vomit, because my torn t-shirt may actually have remnants of omelets on it. From yesterday. I sniff in that secret way people try to surreptitiously look like they are not *so* hygiene-deprived that they don't know whether they're offending half the eastern seaboard.

Damn. I am.

My phone rings. People around me look as I stare at it, slack-jawed. I can see my open mouth in the glass and realize my hair is still in a loose topknot on my head. Is that my nephew's My Little Pony scrunchie?

I really sprinted out the door this morning,

didn't I? Being made an honorary Brony by a seven-year-old with two missing front teeth meant I'd been named "Thparkly Thunthine Auntie Thannon." I smile at the memory.

"Hello?" No one calls me. They always text. And the phone number is new. I don't know this person.

"Shannon, it's me." Amanda. My co-worker. My best friend. My thorn in my side. A ringing phone is an anomaly these days. Most people just zombie text. Me? I have a twenty-four-year-old friend who uses her phone like it's 2003.

"Why do you have a new number?"

"Greg made me get a cheaper plan." Greg is our boss. He makes those crazy coupon queens who buy $400 worth of groceries for $4.21 with 543 coupons look like people from *Lifestyles of the Rich and Famous*.

"Huh. Well, you could have answered the phone when I called this morning and taken some of these bagel hell assignments, you know," I whisper. "I am going to name my reflux Maple Horseradish Amanda after you."

"Oh, thank God! You picked up the jobs."

A very attractive college guy walks in, donning a lacrosse team shirt and a pair of legs that make me wish I were wearing my good underwear instead of my safe underwear. You could go fly fishing in these granny pants.

My eyes can't stop flipping between college dude and Christian Grey. Eight bagel shops, and on the ninth, God gave Shannon a smorgasbord of hot men.

"You took them *all?*" Amanda's voice is somewhere between a dog whistle and a fire alarm. She shakes me out of my head just as Mr. Sex in a Suit walks by, making me sniff the air like an animal in heat. Which I kind of am, suddenly.

He smells like a weekend in Stowe at a private cabin with skis propped against the back wall, a roaring fire in a stone fireplace that crawls from floor to ceiling, and a bearskin rug that feels amazing against all your naked parts.

Even the dormant ones.

Especially the dormant ones.

"On the ninth one right now, but you're blowing my cover," I hiss. "And you *so* owe me. I'm making you pick up those podiatrist evals next month." Podiatrist shops don't exactly feed a sense of sexual desire, so my mind makes me go there. Feet. Hammer toes. *Eww.* Mr. Sex in a Suit leaves through the main doors, coffee in hand.

But wait, I want to cry out. *You forgot to let me lick your cuff links.*

"You can't make me do the bunion walk!" Amanda protests. Yes, mystery shoppers evaluate podiatrists. Doctors, dentists, banks, and even—

"Then you can do all the sex-toy shop surveys," I say, biting my lips after. I can feel the heat from her blush through the phone. Or maybe that's my own body as I lean to the left to search for a glimpse of Mr. Sophistication.

"Bunions it is," she replies curtly. "Come to the office after. We need to talk. Clinching this huge

8

account hinges on how well these bagel shops go." She pauses. "And I am *so* not doing those marital aids shops!" *Click.*

Chapter Two

Nineteen questions compel me to wrap up the rest of my sandwich, throw my half-full latte away, and walk with confidence toward the restrooms, hands shaking from too much caffeine. So what if, in my rush out of the house, I'd forgotten to change out of my yoga pants and torn t-shirt?

I look down. I'm wearing two different navy shoes. Which wouldn't be a problem, except one of them is open-toed.

Whatever. I am fine. This is my last shop of the day. So what if I look like something out of People of Walmart?

Thank goodness Mr. Omelet Cashmere Jacket is gone. He didn't even look at me, which is fine. (Not really, but…) Living in my own head has its privileges, like pretending I have a chance with someone like that. What would he see if he looked at me? Crazy hair, a full figure in an outfit so casual it classifies as pajamas, tired but observant brown eyes, and the blessings of good genetics from my mother, with a pert nose and what Mom calls a "youthful appearance", but I call a curse of being carded forever.

And the whole two-different-shoes thing,

which could be a fashion statement, you know? It could. Don't question it.

The coast is clear. *Tap tap tap.* I knock softly on the men's room door, assuming it's a one-seater like all the other stores I've been in this morning. No reply.

Sauntering in, I do a double take. Damn! Two urinals and two stalls instead of the big old square room. Someone could walk in on me. A guy could come in here and whip it out if I'm not careful.

Then again, it's been so long, I'm not sure I remember what they whip out.

Last year, one of my shops for a gas station chain made me count the number of hairs on the urinal cakes. That was, I contend, the low point in my secret shopping career. Fortunately, this particular chain does not have an obsession with hirsute urinators.

How progressive.

I tap on my phone and open the app, scanning the questions. Enough toilet paper? Check. Faucets in working order? Check. Paper-towel dispenser full? Check.

Toilets and urinals in operating order? Hoo boy.

If you've never been in a men's room, and have only set foot in the ladies' room at most fine (and not so fine) establishments, you need to know this: store owners hate men. No, really—this is the one area where women get treated better. We may earn seventy-seven cents on the dollar compared to men, but, by God, our public bathrooms don't look

Julia Kent

like something out of a Soviet-era prison.

Or worse—a Sochi hotel during the Olympics.

My mind wanders as I try not to touch anything I'm not required to touch in order to do my job and get out of here. I recall the scent of aftershave and man on Mr. Perfect Blue-Gray Suit from a few minutes ago, instead of the acrid odor of moldy cheese, urine, and chemical deodorizer that smells like poison-ivy pesticide. How would it feel not only to touch a man so put together, so confident, so in control—but to be *allowed* to?

The overwhelming pleasure of being in a relationship isn't the actual affection, sex, and companionship. It's the permission to be casual, to reach out and brush your hand against a pec, to thread your fingers in his hair, to hold hands and snuggle and have access to his abs, his calves, the fine, masculine curve of a forearm when you want.

On your terms.

By mutual agreement. The thought of running my palms from his wrists to his shoulders, then down that fine valley of sculpted marble chest to rest on his waist, to slide around and embrace him, makes my mouth curl up in a seductive smile.

That no one will ever see. So why bother?

Besides, I have toilets to flush.

I check the back of the bathroom door for the cleaning chart. You know those pieces of paper on the backs of the doors, with initials and times written on them to verify that the restroom has been cleaned? Someone verifies that verification.

Me. That's who. Of course, I have no way to

verify that JS (the initials down the line for the past four hours) has actually cleaned the bathroom. Only a video camera would be able to tell for sure.

And while modern society loves to videotape everyone in public, mostly for the purpose of catching Lindsay Lohan in an uncompromising crotch shot, corporations haven't begun videotaping bathrooms.

Yet.

And thank goodness, not only for privacy reasons, but because cameras put people like me out of a job. As much as my job drives me nuts on days like this, it's a paycheck. I have health insurance. Paid time off. A retirement plan.

At twenty-four, that's like being a Nobel Prize winner in today's economy. Most of my friends from college are working part-time at retail stores in the mall, being evaluated by secret shoppers like... me.

Question number thirteen stops me cold. "Is the bathroom aesthetically pleasing?" Um, what? It still makes me cringe, even for the ninth time. The walls are a pale gray, with tile running halfway up. Chips and stains on the tile make me wonder what men have done in here. How does taking a pee translate into broken tiles? And those yellowed stains. I shudder. Is it really *that* hard to aim?

Whoosh! Whoosh! I flush both urinals, then rush over to toilet #1. *Whoosh!* I stand in front of the stall to #2 and get ready to flush that one.

I'm in my own little world and let my guard down to ponder the question. I am also exhausted and most definitely not in top form, because I let a few seconds go by before realizing that someone is coming in the bathroom. Out of the corner of my eye I see a business shoe, and that becomes a blur as I scurry into one of the stalls and shut the door.

Heart pounding, I stare at the dented back of the stall door. Then I look down. Chipped red nail polish peeks up at me from my open-toed navy shoe. Aside from being outed as a transgendered man in here, there's no plausible reason why any men's room stall occupant should have red toenails.

I quickly scramble to perch myself on the toilet, feet planted firmly on either side of the rim, squatting over the open bowl like I am giving birth. Because I am genetically incapable of balance—ever—and as my heart slams against my chest so hard it might as well be playing a djembe, I lean carefully forward with one arm against the back of the stall door, the other clutching my phone.

The unmistakable sound of a man taking a whizz echoes through the bathroom. I can't help myself and look through the tiny crack in the door.

It's Mr. Sex in a Suit, his back to me. Thank goodness, because if I got a full-frontal shot right now then how would I answer the "aesthetically pleasing" question from a strictly professional standpoint?

The tiny bit of shifting I did to peer through the crack makes my right foot slip, and I make a squeaking sound, then lose my grip on my phone as my arm flails.

Ka-PLUNK!

15

You know that sound, right? I know, and you know, that I've just dropped my smartphone in the toilet, but he thinks the man—he assumes it's man —in here just delivered something the size of a two-hundred-year-old turtle into the toilet.

I look down. My phone is still glowing, open to the question "Is the bathroom aesthetically pleasing?"

Staying silent, I struggle to remain perched on the toilet and in balance. One palm splays flat against the stall door, one hand curls into a fist as it poises over the toilet water.

Four-hundred-dollar phone

or

Arm in nasty men's room toilet water.

I have the distinct disadvantage of seeing every dried stain on the inside of the rim that my feet occupy, and I know that launching my hand into that porcelain prison means gangrenous death in three days after male pee germs invade my bloodstream and kill me.

But it's a $400 phone.

A *company* phone.

Closing my eyes, I lower my hand into the ice-cold water and pretend I'm Rose in the movie *Titanic*, bobbing on that miraculous door as my hand fishes blindly around the bottom of the toilet for my phone.

I get it not once, not twice, but three times as it slips and catches, slips and catches, and then—

The stall door opens toward me, sending me backwards with a scream, my arm stuck in the toilet

16

as I fall down slightly, my back pushing against the toilet-flush knob.
  Whoosh!

Chapter Three

Mr. Blue-Gray Suit springs into action, jumping into the stall with me and planting nice, big, beautifully-manicured hands under my un-deodorized armpits and lifting me off the toilet. It's like we're in a toilet ballet, my body leaping up above his, suspended for a few seconds, and all I can think is *My arm is dripping toilet water all over a cashmere suit that costs more than my student loan balance.*

My second thought: *This will be one hell of a story to tell at our wedding reception.*

Our eyes lock as the toilet roars, and if we were anywhere else I could imagine this was a waterfall on a deserted island in the middle of the South Pacific, the two of us the only people inhabiting the island, forced by pure survival to have sex like monkeys and procreate to save the human race.

A sacrifice we both suffer through.

Except I'm not on an island with this man, whose arms don't even seem to strain under my size-sixteen weight. My breasts bob as he makes split-second calculations without looking away from me. Somehow, he moves my entire body, which is now on fire from his sure touch and pure, animal strength, and sets me down without either foot falling directly in the toilet.

The pain of the toilet handle digging into my shoulder blade when I fell back is making itself known, and my arm is dripping, but—but!—Mr. Death by Toilet Rescue is looking at me with concern, and almost as good:

I am clutching my phone.

This all took about five seconds, so I'm panting, and the top knot of my already unruly hair has come undone, leaving a curtain of long waves framing my face. The ends of some of it are wet.

Oh, gross. Toilet arm, toilet phone—toilet *hair*?

The first words we share finally fill the air. He initiates with a grin.

"We have better seats out in the dining room, you know."

"My phone needed a bath," I reply, combing my hair with my dry hand, and now it's wet, too. I wonder what I look like right now, but I'm afraid if I look in a mirror I will crawl back into the toilet and try to flush myself out of this mess.

"What, exactly, have you been doing with your phone to make it so dirty?" he asks with a leer.

He steps back out of the stall with a gentlemanly sweep of his arm, green eyes filled with a mixture of mirth and guardedness. As he moves, he reveals a full-length wall mirror, giving me my own nightmare.

Oh. *That's* what I look like. Anyone have a

spare coffee stirrer? Because I could stab myself in the eye and maybe bleed to death right here.

Or embarrassment will kill me. No such luck. If embarrassment could kill, I'd be dead nine times over by now.

I study myself in the mirror. Time seems measured by increments of incredulity, so why not make Mr. Toilet Rescuer think I'm even crazier by looking at my reflection like a puppy discovering "that other puppy" in the mirror? Long brown hair, wet at the ends in the front. Split ends, no less. Who has the money for a decent cut after I needed new tires for my ancient Saturn? My torn pink t-shirt and gray yoga pants make me look like your average college student, except my shoes bring me to a screeching mental halt.

Yoga pants and one loafer, one open-toed shoe make me look like Mrs. McCullahay down the street, dragging her trashcans out to the road at 5 a.m. with mismatched shoes, a mu-mu, and curlers in her hair while an inch-long ash hangs out of her mouth.

"At least I don't smoke," I mutter. Then I remember where I am, and look slowly to my left.

Mr. Smirky Suit leans casually against the scarred, dented stall wall, his face settled into a look of amusement now, but he's not going anywhere. Feet planted firmly in place, I realize he's giving me that look.

No, not *that* look. I'd take that look from him any time.

I mean the look of someone who will not let

me out of here without an explanation.

An explanation I am contractually obligated *not* to give. Outing myself as a secret shopper is *verboten*. Unheard of.

Grounds for termination.

See, the first rule of mystery shopping is like the first rule of Fight Club: don't punch anyone. Oh. Wait. No…it's that you don't talk about it. Ever.

Though, sometimes, that not-punching rule comes in handy, because there are some really weird people in stores.

And Mr. Suit looks at me like I'm one of them.

"Let me introduce myself," he says, taking the lead. His body moves effortlessly from leaning to standing, then he takes two steps forward and I retreat until the backs of my calves hit the toilet rim again. I'm backing away from him and I don't know why.

"Declan McCormick. And you are?" Instinct makes me reach my hand out, and he's clasping mine before we both realize it's the toilet-contaminated hand.

He pretends it's perfectly normal, keeping strong eye contact and pumping my hand like it's the handle to a well. Except his fingers are warm, soft, and inviting, the touch lingering a little too long.

His eyes, too. They study me, and not like he's cataloging my features so he can file a police report or have me Section 35'd for being a danger to myself and others.

I am being *inventoried* in the most delicious of

22

ways.

As a professional whose job it is to inventory customer service in business, I have acquired a set of unique skills—but more than that, I now have a sixth sense for when I'm being detailed.

And oh dear…there goes that flush.

And not the toilet kind.

I realize we're still shaking hands, and his eyes are taking me in. "Uh, Shannon. Shannon Jacoby. Nice to meet you." I find my voice.

He looks around the room and bursts out laughing, a flash of straight white teeth and a jaw I want to nuzzle making me inhale sharply. That laugh is the sound of extraordinary want entering my body, taking up residence low in my belly, and now waiting for a chance to pick china patterns and paint colors to really consider itself at home.

Go away, want. I've banished you.

Want ignores me and settles in, cleaning out the cobwebs that have taken up residence where I used to allow desire and hope and arousal to live.

Squatter.

"Shannon, this has to be the strangest way I've ever met a woman." One corner of his mouth curls up in a sexy little smile, like we're on a beach drinking alcohol out of coconuts carved by Cupid and not in a ratty old bathroom with a fluorescent tube light that starts buzzing like a nest of mosquitoes at an outdoor blood bank.

"You don't get around much, then," I say. My toes start to curl as my body fights to contain the wellspring of attraction that is unfurling inside me.

23

No. Just…*no*. I can't let myself feel this. You spend enough time trying not to feel something and all that work gets thrown away with one single flush.

He does that polite laugh thing, eyes narrowing. I decide to just stare openly and catalog him right back. Brown hair, clipped close, in a style that can only come at the hands of a very expensive salon owner. The bluish-gray suit, textured and smooth at the same time, shimmering and flat as well under the twitchy light. Skin kissed by the sun but also a bit too light, as if he used to spend a lot of time outdoors but hasn't recently.

A body like a tall tennis player's, or a golfer's, and not my dad with his pot-bellied buddies getting in a round of nine holes at 4 p.m. just so they can have an excuse to drink their dinner. Declan is tall and sleek, confident and self-possessed. He moves like a lion, knowing the territory and owning it.

Always aware of any movement that interests him.

I'm 5' 9" and he's taller than me by at least half a foot. Tall girls always do a mental check: *could I wear high heels with him?* Steve hated when I wore high heels, because it put me eye-to-eye with him.

"What are you doing in the men's room?" he asks, smirking at me.

I tuck my phone into the back waistband of my pants. If there's a chance in hell it's still on, he might see the screen and figure out who I am. My wits begin to return to me. A zero-sum game forms in my body: wit vs. a body part that rhymes with

24

wit that starts with C and that stands for trouble.

Wit is losing.

"I must have gotten confused." I fake-rub my eyes. "Forgot to grab my glasses on my way to class this morning."

His eyes narrow further, staring into mine. Am I imagining it, or did his face just fall a bit with disappointment? My heart shatters into a thousand tiny shards of glass that I feel like I just swallowed.

"Class? You're a student?" His eyes rake over me and there's a flicker of comprehension there, like some details that didn't gel are making sense to him.

When you trap yourself into a corner, always take someone else's out when you can. "Sure. Yes."

"What class?"

My heart is still jumping around in my chest like my little nephews at an indoor trampoline park after drinking a full-caf frozen mocha. Now he wants to chat while we stand in front of a toilet? And ask me questions about a class I don't really take?

"Excuse me," I say, gesturing with the grace of a three-legged moose on skis. "While I am certain that meeting over a toilet in the men's room right after my hand has been in places that brothel workers in Mumbai won't touch is scintillating, I would prefer to step out of here and escape *Eau de Urinal*."

"You haven't answered my question." He is immutable. Heat on legs. His pulse shows on his neck, right under the sharp curve of his tight jaw, and I want to kiss it. Press it. Feel it and let my own heartbeat join in.

"I didn't realize I was under your command, sir," I retort, saluting him with a rush of sarcasm bigger than my pent-up frustration.

His eyes deepen as he pivots just enough for me to get past him, our bodies brushing against each other with a heat that seems to treble with each nanosecond. I move into the area around the sinks and grab a paper towel, then turn the faucet on, careful to make sure my fingers don't touch the gleaming metal.

"What are you doing?" Declan asks. *Why won't he leave?* Surely someone dressed so nicely has stocks to broker, people to doctor, or laws to lawyer. Women to wetten. You know.

"Do you have any idea how germy bathroom sinks can be? I always do this," I explain, even as my head screams invective and tells me I don't have to explain anything.

"Nice of you to protect the other patrons."

"Huh?"

"If anything is germy…" His voice fades out into a low sound in the back of his throat. It sounds like something you'd hear in a locker room or at a hunting club. He gestures toward my arm.

Damn. He's got a point. I can't even argue, because he's right—but that never stopped me before.

"Toilet water—clean toilet water, and that one had been flushed before I reached in—is surprisingly sterile."

"Sterile?"

"Okay," I backpedal. "Reasonably clean."

"Are you from the health department?" His question sounds like a threat.

"No."

"You just troll men's rooms and spout microbiology statistics like a professor for…kicks." He says it in that maddening way men have of making everything seem like it's a fact, even when they're really asking a question.

Which was worse: having him think I was Amy from *Big Bang Theory* or just some crazy woman who crashes men's rooms and has a fetish for sticking her hand in the toilet?

(Not that there's anything wrong with Amy.)

I finish washing my hands and turn to grab a piece of paper towel, only to find Declan holding one out for me.

"Aha! So now I understand," I say, nodding slowly as I accept the paper towel and dry my hands. "You're the bathroom attendant. Where's your tip cup? You've definitely earned a little something."

The air tingles between us, and it's not the deodorizer machine spritzing the room. "I've earned a little something," he echoes in a voice loaded with suggestion. It's not a question.

Just then, the door bursts open and Mark J. rushes in, eyes wild and frantic.

He sees me and gasps, making a high-pitched noise that you would expect from a forty-something middle-aged pearl clutcher and not a guy who looks like he last starred on some cable reality television show called *Fast Food Wars*.

"You!" he screeches. "A customer said they saw a woman walk into the men's room. I didn't believe it!"

Declan reaches out for Mark J.'s arm. I lose track of time. How many seconds did it take for this to go from bad to worse? My cover cannot be blown.

"She just wandered in by accident," Declan explains. "Or she has a fetish. We're sorting it out right now." I glare so hard at him the hand dryer spontaneously starts.

"Why is she covered in water?" My sleeve is soaked and the ends of my hair are wet. Mark looks at Declan and sees water spots on his jacket. "Oh!" The sound is so soft I barely hear it, but from the look on Declan's face he hears it, too. His eyes close and jaw tenses. This is a man who is not accustomed to suffering fools gladly.

So why is he even talking to me?

"I see, now. Fetish.... I didn't mean..." Mark J.'s eyes plead with Declan to help explain what is going on, because it's clear from the worker's panic that he has about three different theories, two of which involve me and Declan breaking public decency laws and one of which involves questions about my biological gender.

None of his scenarios, though, involve my dropping a smartphone while completing a mystery shop, so I'm safe.

"I'll leave you two to whatever...it was...you

were doing," Mark J. says as his fingers scramble to open the door and get out.

"What do you think," Declan says, eyes still on the pneumatically wheezing door, "he thinks we're doing in here?"

"Twerking?" My mind races a thousand miles a minute, covering territory from remembering how many toilet paper rolls were in each stall to imagining Declan naked with a can of whipped cream and a bowl of fresh cherries beside the bed to reminding myself I haven't shaved in days.

I am a modern-day renaissance woman.

Maybe my eyes give me away during that nude vision of Declan, because the room rapidly becomes warmer and his eyes go dark and hooded as he takes another step toward me. Two more and we'll touch.

Three more and I could kiss him.

"I don't twerk," he whispers, one hand twitching as if it wants to touch me.

"I don't do any of the things Mark J. thinks I do," I whisper back. And then I cringe, because…

"Mark J.? You memorized his name tag?" One of Declan's eyebrows shoots up, and it's the sexiest look ever, like George Clooney and Channing Tatum and Sam Heughan rolled into one.

"He's…uh…"

"Oh," Declan says, his nostrils flaring a bit, lips tight to hold back a smile. "I see. He's your…" The words go low and Declan makes a few guttural noises and nose twitches that either mean he has a mild case of Tourette syndrome or he's suggesting that I'm doing the nasty with Mark J.

This is where the path diverges in the woods, and I? I took the path most likely to humiliate me.

For the sake of being a professional.

"Yes!" I shout as the door opens and in walks a very confused kid who looks to be about ten years old. He double-checks the main door, then gawks at me, slack-jawed and wide-eyed. I like that. Kids are honest. Declan's all smoke and whiskey with me, teasing and playing with me, and I have been up since 4:12 a.m. being texted by secret shoppers who dropped acid and saw unicorns.

Don't play games with me.

"Yes, that's right! Mark J. and I are doing it," I whisper in Declan's ear as the kid runs back to his table and I work on my own escape. "We do it in the walk-in cooler, right by the salad bins. He lays me out over the break table outside and always throws the cigarette butts in the ashtray away. A true romantic. On uniform delivery day he's right there in the truck with me, careful to keep the apron clean while meeting my needs. Mark J. is the man."

I inch over to the door and sprint out to my car as Mark J., now safely behind the front counter, shouts, "Have a good day!"

Chapter Four

My hands shake as I climb in my unlocked car and rifle under the driver's seat in search of my keys.

I find the giant screwdriver. Yes, that is my "keys." The original key broke off in the lock a few months ago and my mechanic—AKA my dad—stripped out the lock and now I shove a giant flathead screwdriver into the ignition and turn and pray.

That's the closest thing in my life to something being inserted into a hole every day.

The car turns over and I gun the engine. After backing up slowly, the car vibrates as I make a right turn onto the main road and head to the office.

The vibrations aren't from the car, which runs smoothly once you actually get it started. Those are my nerves jangling a mile a minute, my body in some kind of post-urinal shock.

I examine my hand. The toilet hand. And then I lean back and feel a bulge at the base of my back. And not the fun kind.

Dirty hand reaches back and finds my sweaty smartphone. The screen is not glowing, and it seems to have developed a sheen of sweat. Or maybe that's from me. Running from the restaurant to my car was about the most exercise I've had in months.

As the familiar roads come into view and I guide my car on autopilot back to my apartment, I try to unwind the crazy, jumbled mess of threaded thoughts that can't untangle just yet. Hot guy. Hiding in the men's room. Dropping my phone in the toilet. Being caught with my hand in there. Being rescued and dripping toilet juice on Hot Guy.

And that was the good part of the morning.

My phone makes a creepy bleating sound, like baby seals dying at slaughter. The screen flickers like it's the last known electronic signal after nuclear war.

I try to shut it off but it just continues making an anemic whirring sound. This is what robots sound like when they die. The noise will invade my dreams for the next few weeks.

A deep breath will cleanse me. No dice. How about two? Nope. Nuthin'. Ten don't really help. By the time I've tried twenty-three deep breaths, I am home and feeling a little faint, with tingly lips.

Let's not add syncope to my growing list of Very Bad Things That Happen on a Mystery Shop.

I park in my assigned spot next to the trashcans, kill the engine, and slowly bang my forehead against the steering wheel. Twenty-three bangs actually calm me. Dented brow and all. By the time I stop, I feel like I can handle a basic shower.

That's more than I was capable of ten minutes ago. Other than a shower with Mr. Suit.

Julia Kent

Who are you, a voice asks me, *and what have you done with asexual Shannon?*

Sitting out here with my dented head and confused heart won't get me anywhere. Amanda's probably frantically trying to find me, and a search party worthy of a missing Malaysian jet is about to be triggered if she calls my mom.

My mom can be a bit dramatic. A bit. The way Miley Cyrus can be a bit controversial.

I sprint into my house, holding the phone like it's a bomb. My apartment is a garage. Mostly. I live above a two-car garage in a neighborhood right behind a college, a one-bedroom place I share with my sister. It requires actual exertion on my part to enter and exit. Twenty-seven nearly vertical steps get me to my front door. An actual key (as opposed to a screwdriver) opens the front door, and then *bam!*

I'm assaulted by a glaring cat.

My cat makes Grumpy Cat look like Rainbow Brite. If glares could peel paint, I could hire out Chuckles to a paint contractor and quit my job, living off my pet's singular skill.

People who think animals have expressionless faces are like people who can ignore an open package of Oreos.

Not quite human.

Chuckles—who probably started glaring after we named him as a puffball kitten ten years ago— sits primly in front of the door, a sentry serving as witness to some oversight of mine.

With a guilty look, I survey my kitchen, which

33

is the first room you walk into in my apartment. Water dish full. Food dish half full.

Litter box—full.

Ah. "I'm sorry, Chuckles. I was too busy putting my hand down a human toilet today. I've had quite enough of excrement today. But I'll change it anyhow, because if you look at me like that much longer I'll burst into flame and they'll find us in a few weeks, you noshing on my crispy legs."

"You should think about the fact that you say more to your cat than you do to your own mother," Satan says from behind my ficus plant.

I scream. Chuckles screams. I pick up Chuckles and fling him at the plant, which serves exactly three purposes. First, it reveals my stupidity. Second, it makes Chuckles plot my death on a whole new level. And third, it makes my mother sidestep the whole fiasco with the fluid movement of a woman who teaches yoga, leaving her to glare at me with a look that makes me realize exactly where Chuckles learned it from.

"Nice guard cat," my mom says. She holds her purse over her shoulder and keys in her hand. "Before you ask," she adds as I press my palm over my heart, willing it to stay in place as Chuckles' death ray of magnetic harm tries to pry it out of me, "Amanda called and told me she couldn't reach you."

"I've been unavailable by phone for no more than thirty minutes. Thirty minutes! And she sends out the National Guard."

Mom looks triumphant. Marie Jacoby is what all my friends called a MILFF—Mother I'd Like to Flee From. A little too tan, a little too blond, a lot too judgmental. My mother doesn't greet you with "Hello."

"You should" is her salutation of choice.

"You should consider yourself fortunate. Some young girls would be falling all over themselves to have a mother who cares so much," she grouses.

"First off, I'm not a girl. And second, you're right. How about I sell you on eBay as mother of the year? You'd fetch a great price."

One eyebrow shoots up. One perfectly threaded eyebrow, that is. No stray hair can live on Mom's face. She visits the mall weekly and the women at the threading spa not only know her by name, they know her preferred coffee order from the little espresso place next to the escalator.

She peers intently at me, her eyes that luminous sapphire I still envy. I got dad's dirt-brown eyes. "You've met someone," she crows, plopping her oversized fake Prada bag on my scarred thrift shop table.

Which means she is here to talk.

"How do you do that?" I screech, channeling the same inner fifteen-year-old she can conjure at will with just two sentences and one knowing look.

Her eyebrow climbs higher. "So I'm right." She stands and gives my coffee machine an appraising look. It is an espresso machine I'd gotten on a mystery shop for a high-end cookware store. "Make me a coffee and I'll only ask the basics."

"Blackmailer," I mutter, but I know the score. Do this and she'll leave me alone. Argue and I am in for the full hover-mother treatment that makes the NSA look like *Spy Kids*.

I grab the can of ground espresso out of the cabinet above the sink and she makes a guttural sound of reproach. Ignoring her, I fill the machine and make sure there is enough water. Sometimes, pretending she didn't make a noise works.

But not this time.

"Look at the food in your cabinets! Coffee. Sugar and sweetener packets. Ketchup and soy sauce packets. Sample-size cookies. Teeny packages of microwave popcorn."

"I eat a perfectly fine diet, Mom," I mutter as the machine begins to hiss. Or maybe that's me. It's hard to tell.

She waves a perfectly manicured hand dismissively. The nail polish matches a thin line of mauve that runs as a single stripe through her shirt.

"Not for you. For the man you'll entertain! He can't see that. That's not wife and mother material. No woman who makes a good wife keeps a pantry like that!"

"Last week you were Feminist Crusader Mom, telling me how proud you were that I finished my degree and support myself!" This is a well-worn argument. Since she turned fifty a little more than two years ago, and as her friends are all getting to Momzilla their way through their daughters' weddings, Mom has become zealously devoted to finding me A Man.

36

Not just any man, though.

A man worthy of a Farmington Country Club wedding.

Mom's phone rings. "You Sexy Thing" fills the room and Chuckles makes a disapproving sound eerily similar to my mother's. I seize my chance.

"Gotta wash the toilet water off my arm!" I call back as I pad to the bathroom and turn on the shower, drowning out whatever comments she peppers me with. Stripping out of the pajamas I've been wearing for far longer than their shelf life feels like shedding a skin.

The tiny, hot pinpricks of escapism give me ten minutes to cleanse myself and to think. Or not think. Mom chats on the other side of the bathroom door, blissfully unaware that I am not listening. Or commenting. Or responding in any way, shape, or form.

That doesn't stop her.

I turn off the shower spray and hear her shout, "And so that's how Janice's daughter found out her and her husband's toothbrushes had been shoved up the robbers' butts."

Whoa. As I towel off, my reflection opens its mouth and closes it a few times, wondering how I am expected to respond to that.

Some things are best left to the unknown.

As I open the door, a plume of steam hits Mom. "My hair! My hair!" she shouts. I inherited her limp hair and Dad's eyes, which is so totally backwards. Dad has lush hair that my sister, Amy, got—perfect spiral curls that rest elegantly in auburn tendrils against her back. And Mom has those blue eyes.

I look in the mirror and Declan's name runs through my mind, planted there by my subconscious. If I say a word about him to Mom then she'll be planning the wedding and have him in a headlock, demanding a two-carat ring before he can say "Hello."

I walk into my bedroom wearing a towel, and stop short. Clothes are laid out on my bed for me.

"What am I? Four?" I mumble. Then I grudgingly put them on, because Mom does have good taste. The adobe shirt she pairs with navy pants and a scarf I never use looks more stylish than I want to admit.

"I can color code your wardrobe for you, Shannon," she shouts from the hallway as I dress.

"You should start a clothing line. Garanimals for Adults. It would be very popular!"

She takes my comment at face value. "What a great idea! I'll ask Amy what she thinks. Maybe we can do one of those crowd-funding things to raise money for it like Amy does."

Amy is an intern at a venture capital company. *So* not the same thing as Kickstarter or Indiegogo. I don't correct Mom, because it's about as useful as correcting Vladimir Putin about the Ukrainian/Russian border.

"Who was on the phone?" I ask.

"Amanda. She wants you to call her. What's wrong with your phone?"

"I dropped it in a toilet on a shop this

morning."

Mom's face freezes in an outrageous O. "You didn't...*retrieve* it?" The only thing Mom fears more than never marrying off a kid at the Farmington Country Club is germs.

"I stuck my hand in the toilet in the men's room and saved it, even as I flushed!" I say with glee.

She glares at me. Chuckles leaves the room, clearly outclassed. "Men's room?"

I smile. "Where do you think I'm meeting men?"

"Oh, Shannon," she groans, reaching for the espresso I made for her before the shower. It's likely tepid by now, but that's how she likes it. "Have you become so desperate?"

"I know the men's room is a bit—"

"No—the men's room is ingenious, actually. No competition, except with the gay ones." She drinks the entire espresso in one gulp and slams the cup down like it's a shot competition during Spring Break in New Orleans. "I mean, really? On a *mystery shop*?" She says the last two words like Gwyneth Paltrow says the word *divorce*.

"So let me understand, Mom. Trolling the men's room is a clever way to meet a man, but doing so during a mystery shop is debasing?" She quickly pulls my unruly hair into an updo and bobbypins appear in her mouth like she had them shoved up her nose the entire time, waiting for the perfect moment to correct my hairstyle.

"It's just..." She sniffs. "What kind of man

will you meet at a burger joint? Or a car wash? Getting your oil changed or buying a bagel sandwich?" Her face perks up. "Is there an elite level of mystery shopping? Who are the secret shoppers for Neiman Marcus, or the Omni Parker House? What about Tiffany's?" Her eyes glitter. "Now that would be one way to meet the right kind of man."

"The right kind of man." I can't keep the disdain out of my voice, but an image of Declan flashes through my mind. That smile.

"You won't meet him on your eighth bagel sandwich dressed like a college student on the fourth day of exams with a bad case of lice," she adds.

"I don't have lice!"

"Well, honey, you looked like it."

"Mom." I steel myself. "This has been great. Really. But I have to go." I grab my purse and throw a few cups of white rice in a baggie, then shove my phone in it. "But I need to get to work."

"We need to talk, Shannon—"

"Bye! And change Chuckles' litter box for me, would you? He looks like he's about to go in the zen rock garden."

And with that, I run down every one of those twenty-seven steps, grateful for my escape.

Chapter Five

The drive to the office gives my body a chance to settle in to the day. Awake since four a.m., it is screaming for some kind of break.

Or maybe that is my inner thighs. They begin to spasm and ache, and not in that stretchy-groany kind of way after a long weekend of incredible sex.

Squatting on the toilet has, apparently, led to a fair amount of injury. Great. Add this to the growing list of occupational hazards.

If only Declan had been responsible for this burning ache in a decidedly more delicious way. Daydreaming never hurt anyone, right? I let my mind wander, wondering what he looks like out of that suit. In bed. Under bright white sheets on a crisp spring day, windows open and gauzy curtains billowing with the breeze, the air infused with the scent of sensual time.

Would he be a patient lover, taking every curve and valley of my body with a slow touch that built to a crescendo? Or an intense, no-holds-barred bedmate, with fevered kisses and unrestrained hands that need and knead, fusing us together in sweaty promises of nothing but oblivion?

A new kind of ache emerges between my

thighs, and it's closer to the kind I wish I'd had with him.

For the first time since our meeting a few hours ago, I let myself laugh. Really giggle, with belly moving, abs engaged, and chest whooping with the craziness of it all. Was he laughing, too? I feel a blend of incredulity and shame inside me, too, but there's a lot more amusement. Never one to shy away from self-effacing humor, this event will be reshaped and I'll retell it to my friends, crafted in a way that makes everyone think, *That silly Shannon.*

Is Declan even thinking about me at all? The laughter dies inside fast. Maybe I'm just some whacko woman he humored as he now tells scathingly nasty stories to his work buddies about the chubby chick he found squatting on the men's room toilet, fishing her phone out.

Am I the butt of jokes? Does he describe me with vicious derision, using me as a quick one-off story, the office equivalent of a viral BuzzFeed link that makes people pause, point and laugh, and move on?

A lump in my throat tells me I care way too much about what he thinks. Why am I fantasizing about a guy who trapped me in a toilet stall while I was on a mystery shop?

Because you're that desperate, my mother's voice hisses in my head.

I throw an imaginary cat at her.

The company I work for, Consolidated Evalu-shop, Incorporated, is in a building as nondescript as the business's name. If boring had a name, it would be Consolidated Evalu-shop. The building is made of block concrete. The interior steps are concrete as well. No carpeting anywhere, leaving the hallways to echo. If Stalin's army had designed an office building, this is what it would look like.

Fortunately, our actual office has carpet. Cheap industrial carpet that is about as thick as a gambler's wallet the day after payday, but it's carpet. It pads our feet and keeps the floor warm. I open the main door and walk into the office. There is a reception area the size of two or three graves shoved together without any chairs, and then to the right a long hallway, with three offices on either side. At the end of the hall is something the owner, Greg, calls a "kitchen" but I call it a supply closet with a sink in it.

Want coffee? Get it from the donut shop next door. Same if you need to respond to nature's call. Greg doesn't provide fancy fringe benefits like bathrooms, microwaves, coffee machines, or even pens. He uses the freebies he gets at the bazillion marketing conventions he attends (on the company dime, of course).

To be fair, we get plenty of freebies in this line of work, too. You go to enough mystery shops at banks and open a new account, you get to keep your free pens, notepads, water bottles, can cozies, toasters, smartphone cases, and other assorted swag that you receive.

Greg is super-cheap about outfitting the office, but he doesn't skimp on health insurance. I might make slightly more than a full-time assistant manager at the Gap, but I have one hundred percent employer-paid health insurance, so I'm not complaining.

Plus, he pays mileage for all our driving. Which adds up, fast. You drive a piece of junk like I do and you need the fifty-five cents for each mile to feed the hamsters that keep it going.

"Oooh, someone got lucky last night. You're walking like a woman who got what she needed and then some," Josh says, winking as I limp into the office. Josh is the company tech expert, which means we all think he's a little bit shaman, a little bit magician, and mostly a nerd.

My glare should make him spontaneously combust, or at least turn into a hedgehog with a profound case of psoriasis, but no such luck. "Not even close. I hurt my inner thighs sitting on the toilet this morning."

His eyebrows shoot up and disappear into his disappearing hairline. "You need more fiber."

"I need a lot of things, Josh." Limp. Limp. I feel like I've been riding a Shetland pony for three days. At least I don't have saddle sores. But Josh's original idea, of having a man do this to me in bed...Mr. Sexy Suit comes to mind. Not the pompous ass who made me flush my own hand and cell phone, but the one I turned into Mr. Dreamy before The Great Toilet Fiasco of 2014.

I have the second door on the left, sandwiched between Josh and Amanda. My office smells like pine and vinegar, which means it must be Thursday. The cleaning crew came through the night before. I

44

hang up my purse, pull out the baggie with rice and my phone in it and put it in my windowsill to bake in the sun, and flip my computer on.

Amanda's left a note on my desk: *Leave it for two days in a baggie full of rice. If it doesn't work, we'll get you a new one. Greg won't be happy, but too bad. Hope your hand doesn't fall off from germs.*

It's so nice to have a friend who really gets your OCD phobias. Or who understands your mom. Or both.

"Shannon? I recovered your data," Josh says, scaring the hell out of me. He moves like a vampire, suddenly behind you in your office. I think he likes it. Office sadist.

But I forgive him, because *what*? "You recovered my shops?" Hope springs eternal.

"It's all in the cloud now, so thank me for setting that app up and forcing Greg to spend money on something worthwhile. Everything is in there but the last one, because *you* didn't hit save." I get a scowl that makes me think Chuckles is more evolved than most humans. Josh looks like a lamb pretending to be mad.

"I was perched over a men's toilet trying not to watch a man whip it out. Don't you dare shame me."

"The only shame is that you didn't try to look when he whipped it out," Josh says, eyes twinkling.

"You recovered *all* eight shops?" I'm incredulous. This is making my day already, and it's only 11:37 a.m.

He nods. I throw my arms around his neck and hug him. "I would French kiss you if you weren't gay," I murmur.

"You keep this dry spell up and you'll start French kissing me even though I *am* gay," he mutters, shaking his head. "If the only action your inner thighs are getting is while hiding from a hot guy in the men's room of a shop, it's time for a lifestyle evaluation."

"Let's mystery shop Shannon's life!" Amanda squeals, appearing at the perfect moment. The perfect moment to go through another episode of *Let's Dissect Poor Shannon's Failed Love Life*, that is. My mother would emcee it.

We're on season three, episode five by my count. Netflix should pick this one up. People could binge watch and point to the TV as they laugh, feeling a sense of relief while thinking, *At least I'm not as bad as Shannon.*

I could provide an important public service.

"What about Hot Guy? Did he ask for your number?" Amanda and Mom had clearly connected.

"I'm sure he hits on all the women he meets who have their arm flushed down a toilet in the men's room." *Does he?* Because if he's met more than me that way, then it's really not me. It's him.

"Sample size of one!" she chirps. "You stand out from the crowd."

"I'm the only one who could give him E. coli by feeding him grapes!" I look nervously at my hand. It looks the same.

"You didn't catch his name?" Josh asks.

46

I freeze inside. *Declan McCormick* is on the tip of my tongue, but I keep it behind my teeth, like a candy you savor and suck on. Heat creeps up my chest and neck as I think about things on Declan I could suck.

I shake my head hard, like a dog after a swim. "Nope. Just really rich, really confident, and enough of an asshole to make me want him."

All three of us wistfully sigh in unison.

They believe the lie. They should. We're all really good liars. You kind of have to be in this business, because you spend so much time pretending to be something you're not, all while evaluating the surface level of people.

It's a cold job when you think about it that way. Now I frown and Amanda looks at me with concern. Then I realize she has black hair again. Fourth color change in four months.

"What did you do?" I ask as she follows me into my office. Yesterday she was a blonde, and the shift is jarring, like she's gone from looking like a beach bunny to a dominatrix.

"Carole flaked on the hair salon shop, so I had to go to yet another color, cut, and style," she says sadly. She touches the ends of her hair. "I look like Morticia Addams."

I snort. "You look like Katy Perry." Amanda is the cheerleader type. Was in high school, still is. And yes, I'm lying a little, because Amanda actually has near-zero similarity to Katy Perry other than black hair and red lips. In fact, right now, she's staring at me in a creepy way with that new hairdo, like that woman on the *Oddities San Francisco* show.

Like she either wants to tell me a secret or stick me in a jar with preserved three-headed piglets from 1883.

"You got all your shops in?"

"Eight out of nine."

She looks at the wall clock in the hallway. "Twenty-three minutes to get the last one in and we get credit for exceeding client expectations."

"But—um—hello? Toilet water? Dead phone? Hot guy?" I can't catch a break.

"Hot guy or no hot guy, we have that big meeting at four today with Anterdec Holdings, and if we get this all in on time it makes it much easier to land a client so big Greg will have to start turning the heat up over fifty-five in the winter."

"You know how to improve company morale. Don't tease me," I say, pretending to fan my face. "Next thing you know you'll tell me we're allowed to turn the overhead lights on after sundown."

"Don't push it," she says in a fake flat voice. But with the new hairstyle she makes my abs tighten with fear. I flinch. She sees it and frowns.

"You look like something out of a BDSM novel," I explain.

One corner of her mouth hitches up. It's half adorable and half chilling. "Really? Too bad I'm not dating anyone right now. This is just going to waste." Her hand sweeps over her face.

"Ha."

"Twenty-one minutes! Hurry! Once we have

48

all the shops in the system we can do a quality-control check and go to this big meeting with an unblemished record. And then maybe they'll give us the Fokused Shoprite account." Amanda says this with a triumphant grin.

My jaw drops. "We have a shot at sniping one of their accounts?" Fokused, or Foked, as we call them, is our archenemy...er, competition. Consolidated and Fokused are the biggest consumer experience and marketing firms in the city, and the rivalry is strong.

If my little toilet-hand fiasco had cost us this account, I would have not only cried, Greg would have sold my office furniture out from under me and spent the $17 it was worth on coffee for the rest of the staff out of sheer anger.

My computer boots up and I log in to the website interface, a *zing* of thrill flooding my extremities as I see all complete shops from this morning, except that red ninth one.

Incomplete.

Incomplete this, sucker. Ten minutes later, I am stuck with one final question.

"Is the bathroom aesthetically pleasing?" I let my mind drift to Declan, remembering those smoldering eyes, the tightly muscled jaw, how his cheeks dimpled when he laughed. The snug cut of his tailored jacket across those broad shoulders and how strong and sure his hands had been on me, making certain I didn't fall.

Into the toilet, that is.

Can a relationship develop from two people

who meet like this? Am I hopelessly dreaming? Or am I doomed to live the rest of my life surrounded by men at fast food restaurants on $5 sandwich day, or guys opening new accounts at banks to get a free pair of tickets to a big amusement park, or—

I take a slow, deep breath and remember the heat of his fingers on my arm. The warm questions in those eyes. The willingness to laugh with—okay, *at*—me.

I click *Yes* and then submit, ready to perform the killer client pitch of my entire career.

Chapter Six

Amanda and Greg like to pretend that they're the experts at client pitches, but while they're good openers, I've become the closer.

And in business, the closer is everything.

I have this innate sense that tells me how to fine-tune my words and convince a wavering vice president of marketing, or director of consumer relations, or vice president of *let's invent a title for the owner's son*, that Consolidated Evalu-shop, Inc. will help their company usher in a new wave of business that positions them at the vanguard of a paradigm shift in the industry.

See? I'm good.

Marketing really isn't anything more than word salad, and I don't mean the schizophrenic kind. Learning to speak business jargon fluently is definitely an acquired skill.

Growing a penis is another one. Haven't mastered that just yet, though if I could, I would.

You know how many female VPs I meet? Maybe one in fifty. Presidents? One. Ever. A smattering of directors, more assistant directors, and then the glut of "coordinators," which can mean anything from an underpaid, overworked equivalent of a vice president but without the paycheck to a glorified secretary.

And when you walk into a meeting, you have no idea what you're dealing with.

Guess what my title is?

Yep. Marketing coordinator.

"They emailed me this morning," Greg says. I take a good look at him. One thing I have to give to Greg—he cleans up well. He's a little younger than my dad, which makes him mid-forties or so. You know—old, but not ancient. Brown hair, thinning out, and cut super short the way guys who won't quite admit they're balding cut their hair. His wife made him ditch the old 1980s frames he used to wear for a sleek updated look, and his suit is tailored, which it has to be. The beach ball masquerading as a stomach needs to fit.

"Portly" is the genteel term for what Greg looks like. He's a great Santa at Christmas over at the community center, and today he looks like a distinguished gentleman ready to play hardball at the boardroom table.

"What'd they say?" Amanda is wearing a long, gray pencil skirt with a slit up the back. Nothing too racy, but with her curvy hips it looks business sexy. Red silk shell and black blazer. With the black hair and red lips, she has the look down. I have to stop myself from calling her Mistress.

"They want to expand the account by sixty percent. Into their high-end properties."

Amanda and I suppress twin squeals of excitement. Anterdec owns an enormous chunk of real estate, hospitality companies, and restaurants in the area. If they have fewer than two hundred properties, I'd be surprised.

An account this big, including their luxury hotels, fine dining, and elite transportation services, could turn Consolidated into a major player in marketing services for enterprise companies.

(See how I did that? I should be a highly paid copywriter. Instead, I spent the ten minutes after we got here using a lint roller to peel cat hair off Greg's back.)

"You want first dibs on mystery shopping The Fort?" Greg's words make my heart soar. Amanda's eyes open so wide I think one will fall out. The Fort is *the* exclusive waterfront hotel in Boston. Rumor has it the mints on the pillows have mints on them. Sheiks and royalty from around the world stay there when they are in town.

A night in a standard suite costs what I make in a month.

"Dibs!" I hiss. Amanda snarls.

"Down, you two. If this goes through, there will be more than enough shops for both of you and Josh. The luxury shops will be handled in-house. I might need to add employees."

"You might need to add heat and a toilet," Amanda cracks just as the receptionist catches our eye and motions toward the board room.

We are in the financial district of Boston, where people like me notice the nearest Starbucks or Boloco, but folks like the vice president for marketing at Anterdec notice which building has a helipad for helicopter landings.

Three suited men are turned away from us as we enter, their heads huddled in discussion. One head is gray, two are brown.

No women. Of course.

"Advantage already. No women," Greg whispers in my ear. He is the opposite of sexist. He pays all of us, male or female, the same crappy salary.

The office is gorgeous. I'd expected a sleek, black and gray glassed room overlooking the building across the narrow road; the financial district isn't close enough to the water for everyone to get their sliver of a view of the ocean.

But *this*. We are on the twenty-second floor and the window looks out over a rooftop terrace next door, covered with topiary filled with... PacMan?

"Is that a PacMan maze on that rooftop, or am I nuts?" I whisper to Amanda, who stifles a giggle.

"Big video-game development company next door. Their IPO just happened. I hear one of the perks of working there is that they deworm your dog or cat on site while you work."

I open my mouth to say something back, when the three men turn and stand, facing us.

My mouth remains open.

One of the men is Declan McCormick.

His eyes meet mine and five different emotions roil through that chiseled jaw, those sharp eyes, that sun-kissed skin. Most of them are scandalous. All of them make my toes curl.

And then his face spreads with the hottest, warmest, most mischievous smile I have ever seen on a man who has taken over my damn senses, and he says:

"Toilet Girl!"

Chapter Seven

There are so many ways the next few seconds can unfold. I can pretend I don't know what he is talking about and remain professional, giving him nonverbal cues and hoping he is decent enough to play along.

I can turn around and run screaming from the building.

I can laugh nonchalantly and step forward with grace, offering my hand and telling the story with self-deprecating sophistication and wit so overwhelming that I clinch the deal right here.

Instead, Amanda blurts out, "That's Hot Guy?"

Declan's face goes from joyfully amused to ridiculously gorgeous as he tucks his chin in one hand and tries not to laugh. The gray-haired man looks from Declan to me with an annoyed expression, the kind you only see on men who don't like to be left out of knowing the score, and who are accustomed to having everyone make them the center of attention.

The other brown-haired man takes a step forward and offers his hand to Amanda, who is standing a step closer to them than I am. "Hello. I'm Andrew McCormick, and you are…?"

"Amanda Warrick," she says with a clipped, professional cadence. The lingering handshake is mutual, though.

He seems to drop her hand with great reluctance, then turns to me. "My brother calls you Toilet Girl, but I'm going to assume that's a stage name?"

Amanda snickers. Greg looks like I just drop-kicked his Christmas morning puppy out the twenty-second-story window. Declan watches me with deeply curious eyes and a flame of interest that makes the room feel like we've moved to the equator, and the gray-haired man clears his throat.

"You look a bit...flushed," he says to me with a confused smile, but impish eyes. I can see what Declan will look like in thirty years.

The room descends into chaotic laughter.

"Shannon Jacoby," I say, ignoring the howling monkeys and reaching out to shake what I assume is James McCormick's hand. The CEO of Anterdec, I've researched him thoroughly, but never in a million years put the McCormick name together with Declan. Amanda does the personal background research, and I mentally kick myself for not reading her brief. Then again, I didn't exactly plan to have Meghan drop nine shops on me in the wee hours of this morning.

"I take it you two have met?" Andrew says to me and Declan, his hard stare at his brother making it clear he expects the full story later.

"Careful, Dad—you don't want to know where that hand's been," Declan says dryly as the elder

58

McCormick and I grasp hands for a quick shake.

"May I speak with you for a moment?" I ask Declan through a gritted-teeth smile. Anger blazes bright in me, turning a heat that had been uncomfortably sultry into a fiery mix of professional offense and uncontrollable lust.

Declan comes over next to me and places his hand on the small of my back as if to guide me to a quiet corner of the room so I can hiss at him while the others introduce themselves.

We both freeze. The touch of his palm, polite but firm, makes my entire body pulse with electricity and groundedness. His hand represents some core I didn't know I lack. Our breath becomes one, and I will myself not to look at him, because if I do, what will I see in his eyes?

Anything but the same feelings I have right now will destroy me. And the not knowing is easier to live with than certain rejection.

He leans down, hot breath tickling my ear, blowing lightly on the strands of hair that escape my up-do.

"I've been thinking about you all morning," he rasps. A million snappy comebacks flood my mind, but I hold them in check. Deflecting this—this supernova of attraction—can only happen for so long.

Declan and I are at the vanguard of a monumental paradigm shift, all right.

And all the business jargon in the world can't stop me from what fate has in store.

"Toilet water has that effect on men. They

ought to bottle it and sell it at the perfume counter of Neiman Marcus."

He doesn't react. At all. No snort of laughter, no eye roll of derision. Just a heat that radiates off him and makes me simmer.

"What were you really doing in that bathroom?" he finally asks, the hand on my back moving in slow circles. It's the briefest hint of touch, but it makes me lean in to him, and I smell him, a mix of musk, cloves, and sophistication. "You clearly weren't a student on her way to class."

"PlentyofFish.com wasn't doing it for me, so…"

"You're on the market?" Declan asks. "No boyfriend? What about Mark J.? All that sex in the cooler, next to the salad bins."

I am going to scream. "You called me *Toilet Girl* at a business meeting," I say, remembering my anger. All I want to do is to become a puddle of Shannon at his feet and evaporate magically to reconstitute in his bed. Especially if the sheets smell like him. But I am standing here in professional dress, having added a blazer to the outfit my mom coordinated for me, and Greg is staring at us like two giant dollar signs are popping out of his eyes.

"And I'm *Hot Guy*?" His voice has a touch of steel behind the amusement.

He's got me there.

"How about Hot Guy and Toilet Girl get a cup of coffee after this meeting and see what happens?" he asks, pointedly ignoring everyone else in the room.

"You're asking me out at a client pitch meeting?" I ask, incredulous. My career rests on this account. If Greg doesn't get this deal, I'm stuck mystery shopping podiatrists and insurance agents forever.

"Would it help if I confess you're my first?"

"You're a virgin?" I sputter, just as the senior McCormick clears his throat and Declan and I look up, startled. From the Mr. Bill looks of shock on everyone's face, they've heard my last question.

"If we could get back to business," James says, motioning all of us to sit at the large oak table. It easily seats twenty and has carved legs thicker than my thigh. And let me tell you, that means it's nice and big, like something from the Teddy Roosevelt administration.

The entire office reeks of *man*. Thick, brown leather couches and pub chairs. Ornate Persian rugs bigger than the entire footprint of my parents' house. Heavy wood fixtures and Frank Lloyd Wright-inspired glass lamps.

Make that *original* Frank Lloyd Wright designs, most likely.

My face on fire, among other body parts, I sit at the table. Declan takes a seat across from me. My view faces the window, and it's amazing. And the sky is damn nice looking, too.

Greg rambles for five minutes about marketing crap that used to be important to me, but now all I can do is sneak looks at Declan and wonder how on earth I can put the genie back in the bottle. I don't want to be attracted to him. I don't want to be attracted to *anyone*.

My good nights involve cuddling with Chuckles on the couch while I binge watch seasons of television shows on Netflix with my favorite crab rangoon and hot 'n' sour soup takeout from the place down the street. The guy knows me so well he lets me tip him an extra $3 to hop over to the convenience store and get my favorite pint of ice cream.

Now *that's* love. Even if you have to buy it.

This kind of interest in and from a man is deadly. It kills hope. Because here's how it works: I like him. He likes me. We bump uglies in bed. I want to talk about emotions. He wants to talk about anything but. I want a future.

He wants another girlfriend.

See? I can write the script and deliver it done. Lather, rinse, repeat.

Steve dumped me because I wanted a future and he wanted the female equivalent of a hood ornament. Which, as I smooth my shirt over my ample hips, I am not—in Steve's eyes. The woman he turned to after me is poised, well-coiffed, has a master's in public health from Harvard, and comes from a family that was among the original *Mayflower* descendents.

My Mendon roots can't compete.

Why am I thinking about Steve right now? I wonder, though as I take in the surroundings as Amanda steps up and recites statistics about new product testing and upselling by clerks in the Anterdec fast-food chains, I realize why.

Because Steve should be sitting at a table like this. Probably is, right now, in fact. Negotiating some business deal with a group of smirking suits who view every woman they work with as a coordinator.

I watch Declan watching Amanda, and really look at him. He's serious now, eyes tracking the PowerPoint slides as she clicks through, graphs and charts aligned beautifully to nail the entire point of this meeting:

We know our stuff.

You want to improve customer service, cut down on employee theft, help raise retention, and grow your customer base?

Let me lurk in your men's rooms and report back what I see.

What I saw this morning is suddenly staring back with a wolfish look so deep that I feel raw and vulnerable, like our suits, the rugs, the business paraphernalia is all just a prop to cover up the fact that we're primal beings who simply want each other.

This is new.

This is too much.

Someone says my name. They say it again. Then I feel a massive pain in my ankle.

"Ow!" I utter. Amanda's glare is even sharper than her ankle as it crashes into mine again. She's kicking me.

"It's your turn, Closer," she whispers. I look around the table. James, Andrew, and Greg look at me expectantly.

I stand, completely rattled. The deck I prepared is on the same laptop Amanda's been using, but it's like I've lost all organizational capacity in my mind. Declan won't stop looking at me like that.

Like *that*. Like he's watching me naked and he's nude and rising up to meet every square inch of my...

James starts to frown while Andrew gives Amanda a knowing look. I clear my throat, but before I can say anything, Declan interrupts.

"We have another meeting to get to," he says.

"We do?" Andrew interrupts, then, "Ow!" I get the impression Amanda's not the only one kicking ankles, because Declan gives his brother a fierce look.

"We do. And as the new vice president of marketing, I'm the decision maker here, right?" He looks at James with a hard stare.

All the friendliness drains out of the room. Greg looks like he's about to throw up, then pastes on a sad smile.

"Is there a reason why you won't have me finish the presentation?" I ask, my voice spiked with ice. If he's going to be an asshole and cut me short, and this has all been some kind of game, I'm not leaving without having my say. I've been through enough presentations like this to know that if you can get the senior executive on board, even if the other two don't like it, you have a fighting chance.

"Oh, you'll finish it." Declan's voice is dismissive. It makes my jaw ache, and I bite my tongue. "But I can't now." He becomes a smartphone zombie, avoiding eye contact. He's blowing hot and cold like the old heater in Greg's office.

James stays quiet. I get the sense it's not his normal state. His eyes flick over me, then back to Declan. "Of course, it's your call."

"But my presentation has some hard data that could really affect your decision," I say. I'm not going without a fighting chance.

"I'd like to reschedule your presentation," Declan says as he strides toward the door. Andrew follows him, slowly and with the stance of someone who is not accustomed to being the follower.

"When?" Greg asks.

"Tonight. Shannon and I will have a dinner meeting. Seven. Wear something nice," he says over his shoulder as he walks out.

Fury washes over me and I stand, crossing the big room in seconds. My hand reaches out for his shoulder and he turns around, eyes cold, looking down on me.

"You can't just order me to go on a date with you!" I cry out. The receptionist cocks her head, listening.

"Who said anything about a date?" His face is inscrutable. "It's a business meeting. Leave your address with Stacia and she'll have a driver sent to your home."

And with that, he stalks out. I start to follow him, but Amanda and Greg appear.

"He can't do that!" I sputter to Greg. *Back me*

up, dude, I think.

James McCormick comes out, a bemused look on his face as he stares at me. "Ms. Jacoby, I assume you can give a good show for Declan tonight?"

Show? What am I now? Who cares about this stupid account? I've been turned into a boy toy in seconds by Mr. Asshole in a Suit, and I'm about to give the McCormicks a piece of my mind.

Greg pipes up, finally. Good. *Here we go, boss. Defend me.*

"Shannon would be delighted. I'm sure Declan will love whatever she shows him tonight."

And with that, James McCormick leaves us, disappearing back into the football-field office.

I spin in outrage to Greg. "Thanks for pimping me!"

He shrugs. "The guy said *business* meeting. If that's what it takes to land this account, you can talk about process flow and customer satisfaction over candlelight, right?"

"You ever been told by a VP of marketing to 'wear something nice' and had a limo sent to your home for a *business* meeting?"

Silence.

"Look at it this way," Amanda says, slinging her laptop over her shoulder and shooting me a sympathetic look. "It has to be better than the way you met for the first time."

"And you!" I hiss. "'Hot Guy'? Seriously? You just…I don't even know you people. It's like you've become my mother!"

They both shudder. "That's kind of low, Shannon," Amanda mutters as we walk to the elevator. Greg scurries over to Stacia the receptionist and I hear him giving her my address. My God. It's like my mother has been tutoring him.

"And whoring me out to the VP of Anterdec Industries isn't?"

"I'm sure he won't do anything inappropriate," Greg says as he catches up to us.

"Bummer," Amanda says.

Greg's turn to look outraged. He's old enough —barely—to be our father, and while most of the time he acts like a peer, this isn't one of those moments. A paternalistic air fills the space between the three of us. It's more what I'd expected back in that meeting, and I would have appreciated it then, but I'll take what I can get.

"You absolutely do not need to go to this business dinner tonight," he says, resolute. Amanda's neck snaps back with surprise at the firmness of his words. "I'll go instead."

"Wear something nice," Amanda chirps.

He scowls. My stomach sinks. I want him to say that, but I don't want him to follow through. Being alone with Declan on a date—er, business dinner—sounds like heaven. This is my big chance to prove I am more than Toilet Girl. More pragmatically, if we can mix business and pleasure, why not snag a multimillion-dollar account, too, while I am at it?

The entire conversation taking place in my head makes me need a shower to wash off how dirty

I feel and to need a shower with Declan. *Mmmm*, Declan in the shower, soaping me up, and—

"See how distraught she is!" Greg whispers to Amanda. "Look at that blank stare."

Amanda snorts. "I think she's drooling, Greg. That's the look of a woman dreaming about Hot Guy."

He looks offended. "Why would anyone be... you women are so...I don't understand..." We climb on the elevator and he pushes the *Close Doors* button. He's still sputtering when we hit the parking garage level where his car is parked. "And besides, what do you think your mother would say if she knew?"

"She'd offer me up just like you did, Greg. And go home and cut an extra foot up the slit of any dress I have. She's a better pimp than you when it comes to dating a billionaire."

"He's not a billionaire," is all Greg can come back with.

"He will be when he inherits his share of Anterdec." Amanda speaks with the authority of someone who has snooped through every nook and cranny of a man's Google results.

A dizzy wave of overwhelm makes me cling to the iron-pipe bannister of the concrete steps near Greg's car. "A billionaire?" Mom would get her Farmington Country Club wedding and more if I...

STOP!

"You feeling faint, Shannon?" Greg pauses, looking at me intently. "You seem fragile today." A look of sheer horror passes over him while I

68

struggle to keep down my bites of all those early-morning bagel sandwiches. "You're not...you couldn't be...you know?" He mimes a basketball in front of his already-basketball-sized belly.

"What? A sumo wrestler?" Amanda mimics with startling brutality.

"Pregnant," he whispers. The two of them look at each other with twin expressions of shock and dissolve into hooting laughter, the kind where you wipe your eyes and hope you don't pee your pants.

"Not funny," I say.

"We know. You can't be pregnant. It would be the immaculate conception," Amanda squeaks.

My dizziness passes. "Done making fun of me? Let's get going."

They compose themselves and Greg beeps his car to unlock it. We climb in. I take the front seat and Amanda grumbles. I summon a Chuckles-worthy glare and she cowers, climbing in without another peep.

"What's your rush?" Greg balks as I tap my foot impatiently.

"I have to find something nice to wear tonight."

Chapter Eight

"You snitch!" It's 6:45p.m. and I am being held hostage by terrorist extremists with a list of demands that make Al-Qaeda look like preschoolers playing pirate.

"I didn't mean to tell her," Amanda insists. "She asked me about Hot Guy and—"

"I can hear you. I'm two inches from your mouth," Mom says, waving an eyeshadow wand like she's conducting the Boston Pops. Occasionally it actually hits my eyelid. She won't admit she needs bifocals; her glasses are pushed so low on her nose they might as well be in Albany.

She can't see a thing, and I'm rapidly fearing I look more like Pennywise the Clown than Olivia Wilde. Mom promised me she could make me look like her, or Scarlett Johansson, or Jennifer Lawrence with enough time and high-end makeup.

Right now I'd settle for retaining full vision in my left eye, which she has now poked twice with the eyeshadow wand.

"You have to look good to catch a billionaire's eye," Mom says. Then she frowns and, Lord have mercy, puts down the eyeshadow wand.

"I know," I simper.

"What about the rest of you?" Her eyes comb over her work so far. I think she'd like to produce the Mona Lisa, but is going to have to settle for Lisa Simpson.

"The rest of me? I shaved my legs and armpits. Plucked my eyebrows—"

"Is that's what's different? What did you use, honey? A weed whacker?"

I look at her. She flinches. I swear the corners of Chuckles mouth turn up a tad.

"You can leave now," I say for the umpteenth time. "It's a business dinner."

"Did you shave...you know?" She points vaguely at my crotch area.

"My knees? Yes." I'm playing dumb on purpose.

"No! Your pink bits."

I choke and cough uncontrollably. I am not having this conversation, am I? Seriously? What did I do in a past life to deserve this? I was Eva Braun, wasn't I?

"All the girls your age do it. You'd think having a pubic hair or three was some kind of social crime." She's talking, and the words are coming out, but I can't hear her over the lambs screaming in my head. "Then again, men your age have come to expect a smooth Chuckles, so..."

Chuckles arches his back, the hairs rising on end, and he opens his mouth, hissing.

"A smooth what?"

"Chuckles," she whispers, enunciating the word. He hisses at her.

Julia Kent

"Huh?"

"P-u-s-s-y," Mom spells out. "That's the word your father likes to use now that we need to spice things up in the—"

"Hari-kari! Give me a kitchen knife!" I shout just as my sister, Amy, walks in the door.

"To kill Mom, or you?" She's carrying a bag of groceries and an extremely large foam hand.

"Either. Both. Mom was just telling me *allllll* about how Dad likes to talk dirty in bed."

Amy blanches. "Mom? Boundaries! Please!"

"What? It's not like that time I told you about needing a new diaphragm because it kept slipping during sex and making those strange sucking sounds."

I think even Chuckles turned pale at that one.

Mom keeps going. "Your father said the sounds reminded him of Darth Vader. So then we had this whole role-play thing going on with Princess Leia and Han Solo…."

My cell phone rings with a text. Sweet Jesus, thank you. Saved by the limo driver. "Gotta go!" I say. "What's with the foam finger? You got a date with Robin Thicke?"

Amy gives me a look like a dog having its eyes poked out by a toddler. "Where are you off to?" She tosses the foam finger at Chuckles, who flees. She never answers my question, though, because Mom decides to be the town crier.

"Shannon has a date with a billionaire!" Mom exclaims.

"Oh? And I'm engaged to the leprechaun from

73

the Lucky Charms cereal!" Amy replies, clapping her hands with fake glee.

I'm out the door before I can hear more.

Except the limo driver isn't who greets me when I get down my twenty-seven steps in high heels made of what feel like five-inch hatpins.

It's Declan.

Mom insisted I wear a little black dress, with an emphasis on "little." I'm a DD up top. Her spaghetti-strap ensemble left the equivalent of Girl Scout badges covering my boobs.

My tailored blazer with scalloped edges works well. Mom's borrowed diamond necklace and earrings make the picture. As long as I don't twist an ankle or take out a small pet with my high heels, I should be fine.

Declan is wearing what looks like a tuxedo, but without the tie. He approaches, and there's a moment where the setting sun is behind him and frames his body, the hues of rose and violet streaking the gray sky. He saunters toward me with a look of total absorption, eyes only on me, hungry and appreciative. My core tightens and fills with an unfamiliar feeling.

Desire.

He reaches for my hand and just holds it. He smells like soap and cloves and aftershave. I want to taste him. He looks like he wants to devour me.

"Hello!" says someone from behind me. I close my eyes and wince as my mother breaks her *You should* rule and calls down to us from the top of my stairs. "You kids have fun."

"It's not the prom, Mom," Amy shouts through my open apartment door.

"Of course it's not," Mom snaps. "Shannon had those really bad cramps that night and her date got lice, so it's not like she ever even went!"

Amy's face appears at the door for a fleeting second before she drags my protesting mother inside. *Slam!*

I blink three or four times, silent. Declan's thumb begins to move back and forth, slowly, maddeningly, like it's gentling a spooked horse.

His hand is shaking a bit. Not from nerves.

Because he is laughing.

I jerk my hand away, remembering myself. This is a business meeting. Business. Pure business.

"I promise I don't have lice," he says.

I almost snap back, *And I don't have my period right now*, but I already want to crawl into a hole and die. Why add to it?

"Not having lice is a great quality in a VP of marketing. Especially since so many of them are louses."

"Ouch."

"Hey, I aspire to be one someday."

"Shannon Jacoby, head louse." His face hardens as he realizes what he's said versus what he clearly meant.

"That just sounds all kinds of wrong, Declan."

"How about we both stop talking and just get in the limo." It's not a question. His hand lands on the base of my back and we both freeze again. Electricity travels in a full circuit between our two bodies. His pulse becomes mine. The tiny hairs on the wrist I can see stand up slowly, as if summoned, just like—

Well, just like something else on his body, I imagine.

The hand on my back slides up my spine, over the fine wool of my jacket, sinking into my loose hair, respectful but sending one hell of a signal. There is no pretense here. I don't have to guess whether he's interested. And my signals are so clear that the only way I could be more obvious would be to rent a billboard and hang a twenty-foot color photo of myself naked with the caption "I WILL SLEEP WITH YOU, DECLAN."

It can't be this easy, can it? My mind spins as his fingers move along the tender skin of my neck, making me gasp. I'm looking up at him and his lips look soft. Tender. Commanding and tasty.

A distant sound of ringing glass fills the air. It's distinct and cuts through the spell between us.

Declan looks back toward my front door. My mother is standing next to the open window with a wine glass and a spoon, gently chiming it like she's at a wedding reception and calling for the bride and groom to—

"Kiss! Kiss! Kiss!" she chants.

Declan looks at me, and with a deadpan expression says, "I think your mother wants us to take this nice and slow."

Amy yanks Mom out of the window and I hear muffled yelling. I grab Declan's hand and pull him to the limo door. The driver opens it and I climb in so fast and so inelegantly I hear my skirt split up the seam in the back.

Declan hears it, too, but sits back in the beige leather seat and ogles the vast expanse of creamy skin my mishap now exposes. A scene from a movie I saw recently, where a couple has sex in a limo, the woman in a ball gown, straddling the man, picks this exact moment to make a re-entrance into my psyche, plaguing me.

"Nice legs," Declan says.

"I'll bet you say that to all the marketing coordinators." He starts to say something, and I add, "And to none of the marketing vice presidents."

He thinks about that for a second and says, "You got me there."

Chapter Nine

Our eyes lock.

"Where are we going?" It's a relief to make simple small talk.

He names a restaurant I've always wanted to try, but needed to date a billionaire to afford.

Oh.

"Sounds good," I say, nodding. Leaning back against the buttery leather, I try to take in my surroundings without looking like a major gawker. The leather seats hug my body better than any knockoff Tempur-Pedic memory foam like Mom and Dad have on their bed back home. A small fridge and a few decanters of what I assume are spirits dot the edges of the enclosed space. The limo looks like it could seat six comfortably, eight in a pinch.

With just two of us in here, there's plenty of room to stretch out.

Go horizontal.

Or straddle.

I close my eyes, willing the sensual images that flood my brain to stop. Declan's steady breath doesn't help, cutting through me like he's syncing it with the pictures in my mind. The scent of him fills the air between us and I feel charmed.

And doomed.

Declan chooses to say nothing, just watching me as if it's the most natural thing in the world. His eyes take me in and I wonder how I appear to him. Loose, long hair. Makeup mostly where it's supposed to go. A curvy body in a dress meant to ooze sophistication. A tailored, feminine blazer that says I might be sexy underneath, but I'm all business on the outside.

My inner world is crumbling, brick by brick, and Declan's holding the sledgehammer that demolishes me. Women like me don't ride in cars like this. We don't get invited out for a dinner—business or pleasure—by men like Declan. And we certainly don't entertain wild ideas about happily ever after with men who will go so high in the business world that women like me are just, well... coordinators.

Whatever delusions I hold inside about his attraction for me are there only because he's looking at me like he really means it. As if I am as beautiful and desirable as his look says.

He's very good at pretending that I'm worth the attention.

His phone rings, making me jump. His breathing stays the same, and his sleek, fluid movement impresses me. Nothing seems to rattle him. With dulcet tones, he talks to someone named Grace, the cadence of their conversation quickly familiar to me. Scheduling helicopters and private jets may be out of my realm, but I know a logistics talk when I hear one. Grace is probably his executive assistant. Something about New Zealand, a reception, and then a return flight to the west coast pops up through their twenty-minute conversation.

I spend the time willing my heart to stay in my chest.

If I weren't such a cheap date I'd knock back a shot of whatever is in the crystal decanter at my elbow, an amber liquid that looks good. But two drinks and I'm quite tipsy. Three and I'm drunk.

Four and I'm singing "Bad Romance" at full blast in a really cheesy karaoke performance. Whether there's a karaoke machine or not.

Declan shoots me apologetic looks every so often, and I just smile without teeth. A shrug here and there helps communicate that it's okay. I get it. And I do.

In fact, the phone conversation helps me to bring my overwrought self back to center. Business. This is business. I'm not on a date with him. We're talking about a few million dollars a year that his company wants to spend for a specific value premise, and my company would love to receive that money to offer services.

That's it.

This is a transaction. Not a relationship. And certainly not an affair.

"It'll be at the restaurant?" Declan murmurs into the phone, then his face goes neutral but the skin around his eyes turns up a touch, like a smile without his lips moving.

Grace says something. Declan replies, "Good,"

and hangs up abruptly. It would be rude if it weren't shorthand. I'm sure Grace is doing a dance she and Declan know all too well, keeping the ship running smoothly through the careful discarding of unnecessary social expectations for the sake of ruthless efficiency.

He tucks the phone inside the breast pocket of his suit jacket just as the driver slows the limo, bringing it to a gentle halt. I look out the window. We're here.

Except the entrance we use is most definitely not one for the *hoi polloi*. Wouldn't want the unwashed masses rubbing elbows with the richie-riches, right? My own bitterness surprises me, and I have a hard time looking at Declan for a minute or two.

His eyes shift; he sees it, and wants to say something, but doesn't. Instead, the driver opens my door and Declan's hand comes out to take mine.

My heart seizes with the touch of bare skin on bare skin. Jesus. If the man can get me this close to an O holding my hands, I'll stroke out if we ever make it to a bed, naked.

And there I go again…what is wrong with me? I don't do this. I don't think like this. Not only do I not randomly strip strange men naked with my mind and have little porno movies in my head about them, I don't even think about one-night stands.

The only guys I've ever slept with were friends first. Good friends. The slow, leisurely meandering to physical affection and something more, carefully measured out and talked through is more my speed.

I like to take things slow. To reveal myself layer by layer to men. To dip a toe in the water and pull back. I'm the kind of person who gets into a pool one inch of flesh at a time, pausing to shiver and acclimate.

Declan is the sexual equivalent of doing a cannonball. At 4 a.m. In March in northern Vermont.

As I climb out, my torn skirt shows so much thigh I might as well have given birth.

Declan's eyebrow arches with appreciation. Controlling my breathing is becoming a second job. I stand and he reaches for me again, his hand on my back, and he smells like cloves, cinnamon, and tobacco. Not cigarettes, though.

"Do you smoke?" I ask as he leads me to an enormous oak door that opens suddenly, a concierge standing there in full tux.

"No. That's Dad's pipe you smell. We were working late at the office."

It's cardamon and Bengal tea spicy yumminess. I want to brew him in hot water and drink him.

We enter a room with an arched ceiling so high I expect to look up and see God with his finger outstretched. The dusky night shines through rounded windows at the peak. Dark mahogany covers the walls and muted lighting gives the restaurant a womblike feel. I can see past the front desk into the main dining room, where thick burgundy curtains frame each table.

This is a place designed for privacy.

"Ms. Jacoby." The maître d' appears, a man who looks to be about my father's age, with gray hair and a salt-and-pepper goatee. He's shorter than Declan, but lean, like a triathlete. Dressed in a tuxedo slightly different from the man at the door, he exudes luxury and service.

In his hand is a small white box with a bow and a gold paper medallion on it. He holds it out to me.

Puzzled, I look at Declan, who just smiles. I slide my fingernail along the gold seal and open the box.

It's a corsage.

"What?" A sentimental laugh fills me, and suddenly I'm at ease.

"You missed your prom, so I thought..." Declan has been calm, cool, and collected until this moment. Right now, he looks like a nervous seventeen year old, though he covers it quickly, eyes going back to a hooded, careless look quite fast.

I pull it out of the box and pin it to my blazer. It's a tasteful set of small red and white roses with a sprig of baby's breath around it. Simple. Elegant.

Special.

I stand on tiptoe and kiss his cheek. My lips graze his jaw as I step down. He's clean-shaven, but the rasp of my skin against his makes my entire body fill with instant lust.

"This is the nicest gesture anyone has ever done for me at a business meeting. Normally I'm lucky to have my own laptop outlet." I can't say what I really want to say, a mixture of gushing gratitude and joy that my babbling adolescent self is screeching inside. The words *Thank you* and *He likes me!* echo a thousand times a second through my mind and heart.

The box disappears as if the maître d' were Dumbledore with a wand, and he leads us back to a table for four, shrouded on three sides by thick velvet curtains, a dim chandelier above us.

Declan pulls my chair out and I sit, scooching in, the press of cool leather a surprise on my upper thighs. Damn. My skirt's split that high?

I'm unnerved again. A corsage? The heady scent of roses and caring fills the air around me. Declan's looking at me with eyes that say this is *not* a business meeting, and my body responds to him like it has to no other man. Ever. Not even Steve made me feel like this.

"I didn't go to my prom either," he says as we settle in. A waiter fills our water glasses and a bottle of wine appears. Before I'm asked, a glass of red is poured for me.

I hate red wine.

"I would have thought that you were prom king," I say.

He shakes his head, eyebrows furrowed. Then he waves a hand as if dispersing a bad memory.

"What?" I ask. I feel bolder now, as if I have the right to make him tell me whatever it is he was about to dismiss.

"I...I missed it because of my mother," he says, reluctant, as if the confession is against his nature.

"Your mother?"

"She was in the hospital."

My mind races to recall all the details Amanda and I learned when we researched Anterdec after our meeting. I know the name is the amalgam of the three sons' names: Andrew, Terrance, and Declan. An Ter Dec. But Mrs. McCormick…I don't remember anything about her.

"She died the day after my prom," Declan says softly. Our eyes meet, and mine must be horrified, because he reaches out for my hand to comfort *me*. He's the one whose mother died.

"You lost your mother that young?" I can't help it. My throat fills with sympathetic tears. My mom may be a pain in the ass, but I don't know what I'd do without her.

"It's been ten years," he says thickly. "But thank you."

"For what?"

"For reacting like that."

"Like what?"

"Like you care. Most people don't let themselves have genuine reactions to anything emotional."

"I'm not most people." The words come out wrong. What I want to say is *I wear my heart on my sleeve,* but that seems too vulnerable. This is just a business dinner, right?

Right.

"I'm sorry," I say, pulling my hand away with great reluctance. He squeezes it and begins to run his thumb along the soft skin of my wrist.

He's not going to let me retreat.

"So tell me why you need more convincing to give this account to Consolidated," I say, trying to change the tenor of this encounter.

I fail.

"Tell me why you're so afraid of me."

I reach for the red wine with my open hand and twirl the glass. The last time I drank red wine was with Steve, at our final work outing for him. He dragged me along to a big dinner with his firm and I choked down a glass and a half as he sent me a million nonverbal signals throughout the entire dinner.

Most of which involved scowls and eye rolls, because I did everything wrong.

Declan takes a sip of his wine and returns his attention to me.

"I'm not afraid of you." I really want white wine. A battle inside emerges. *Let it go*, one part says. *Speak up and assert yourself* says another. *Billionaire grandchildren* says my mother's voice.

I take a big sip of the red wine and choke it down.

"Maybe you're afraid of yourself," he says.

"Maybe I'm afraid you think I'm just being whored out by my boss so I'll land this account."

"Maybe I don't need sex so badly I trade accounts for it."

"Maybe that was never an option."

"Maybe I'm more interested in knowing why you were perched on that toilet. You still haven't answered my question from earlier."

That makes me laugh. "Why do you think? I was finishing the last mystery shop of the day. Who do you think reports on the cleanliness of the bathrooms?"

That makes him pause and take another sip of wine. "Never thought about it." He's still holding my hand, but his thumb stops moving.

"Of course not. That's *my* job. Not yours." I lean in, lowering my voice. "And thank you for not asking me to count the pubic hairs on the urinal cake."

"You're welcome, I guess." He does a double take. "Our competitors do that?"

"And worse. Don't ask what I have to do when I evaluate a manicure salon and detail their anti-fungal procedures."

He closed his eyes, but he's amused. "How romantic."

"I wouldn't talk like this if we were on a date. But this is all business."

We both look at our clasped hands. Then our eyes meet and he starts to say something, but the waiter appears and introduces himself. A flurry of recited specials and then we order. I get the filet and Declan orders some complicated pheasant dish.

"No salad and fish?" he asks when the waiter leaves. We've dropped hands. It feels weird to be disconnected. We're sitting next to each other, yet the table is large.

"Was I supposed to? Is this a mystery shop and that's the required meal?" I'm teasing, but it occurs

88

to me that this is the first time I've dined out in a long time where I get to choose exactly what I want.

He cocks his head and studies me. In the low light of the restaurant, I can see auburn highlights in his hair. "Tell me about your life."

"Wow. You start small, don't you?"

He smiles wide, flashing those perfect teeth. "Tell me."

"I'll tell you about the account," I insist, trying hard to bring this back to business.

He sighs. "You *have* the account."

"I do?" I squeak.

"Of course. Now I want more."

Chapter Ten

"Wait. Why did you ask about salad and fish?" First things first.

"Because that's what every woman I date orders when we dine."

"Seriously? There's a meal code? I'm breaking some rule by getting *beef*?"

"You ordered what you like. I find that appealing. No pretense. No affect. You're just being Shannon."

Which wasn't enough for Steve. "I'm being the marketing coordinator for Consolidated Evalu-shop, Declan. You've just told me we have the account. Thank you."

Deflect deflect deflect.

"No—thank *you*. Once I realized what you were doing in that men's room, I knew we needed to give your company the account."

I almost drop the wine glass in shock. A tiny splash of red wine stains the white tablecloth. It looks like blood. "You knew who I was?"

"Not quite. I figured you were with Consolidated, though. We knew your company would perform shops this week. It's one of the reasons I was there. Just spot-checking stores."

"And you didn't say anything?"

"I said a lot of things. You kept your cover as much as possible. Even to the point of hilarity."

"And embarrassment."

"That, too."

"Most people find me uncouth." Okay, *Steve* found me uncouth. Why am I thinking about Steve right now? I should be pretending to need to use the ladies' room and running in there to frantically text Amanda and Greg the good news.

"Anyone who thinks that is an ass who doesn't know an authentic human being from a blow-up doll girlfriend."

"I never said anything about a boyfriend," I protest.

"You didn't have to."

I am torn between being offended and being attracted to him, the professional in me screaming that this is inappropriate, but the woman inside wanting to press myself against him and explore.

All I can do is make a funny whimpering sound of defeat and confusion.

A flicker of movement in the corner of my eye catches my attention. A couple has come in to the restaurant, the woman with long, straight blond hair that reaches the cleft of her ass. She's willowy thin and wearing a tight white dress with a bright red silk sash as a belt. Her date is bent over, face out of sight, but I stiffen as I recognize the body, knowing those broad shoulders, that nipped waist, and the cut of the Armani suit with the fraternity pin at the lapel.

And then Steve stands up and looks into the dining room. Craning his neck, he's playing the room, searching for someone he can network with and impress. Building a client base is important, he always said. But who you run into a dinner or a bar or the gym is worth so much more. His eyes land—

Directly on me. His face turns to the right as if he can't believe he sees what he sees. His hand on his date's waist tightens, like he's saying *I'm taken*.

No shit, Sherlock.

Declan follows my stare and his eyes narrow. He reaches for my hand again. Predatory. Like he's claiming me. Staking out his territory.

Maybe, Steve, I'm taken, too.

"Who is that?" Declan asks.

I watch as Steve's eyes move over to Declan. Instant recognition kicks in. Steve is an opportunist at heart. He appears to know exactly who Declan is, and this is a script I can write, too.

"That's my ex," I say without moving my lips.

"Good ex or bad ex?" he mutters. I break away and stare at Declan now, because what kind of man gets the landscape of dating *that* well?

"Social climber ex. Mendon girls aren't his thing. He traded up for a nicer model," I whisper, my insides going cold.

Declan shifts his chair a tiny bit closer to me and says through a serious expression, "Don't do that."

"Do what?" Steve and his date are still chatting with the maître d', though Steve points to us. Her eyes light up when she sees Declan, and she chats animatedly with Steve.

"Let him dictate how you view yourself."

I snort. "Like it's that easy."

"It can be."

"It can be," I mimic. I reach for the wine glass and chug it all down in a few gags.

"If you let it, Shannon." His eyes are serious.

"Why did you go all cold billionaire at the end of the meeting earlier today?" I ask. What do I have to lose? Might as well just give in and be me at this point. My day started in the crapper, and as Steve walks slowly across the enormous dining room toward us, it looks like it's ending with a piece of shit.

"Because I learned a long time ago that it's better to have people react to *you* than to react to *them*."

Stunned, I sit and ponder this, his words reverberating in my head as Steve appears, gushing and complimentary.

"Shannon! What a wonderful surprise!" Steve's doing his best Tim Gunn impression. "Don't you look fantastic!" Air kisses follow as he bends down and awkwardly embraces me. I get a mouthful of blue wool lapel.

His date looks like she just ate a lemon.

"Jessica Coffin, this is..." Steve pauses. Declan's hand clasps mine hard. "...an old friend, Shannon Jacoby."

Old friend? All righty, then. If you call the woman you went shopping for engagement rings with and fucked for the better part of two years an "old friend"...

I don't stand. She reaches out and shakes my hand with a cold salmon she pretends is a palm and fingers. Coffin is an old New England/*Mayflower* family name. It fits her.

Steve looks at me, then Declan, then me, then Declan, clearly expecting me to introduce them. His eyes land on our clasped hands.

I've never seen a coyote at the moment its ears pick up the sound of doomed prey, but as I watch Declan watching Steve, I feel like I'm pretty close right now. It's like *When Animals Attack: Boston Brahmin Brawl*—coming soon on The Learning Channel, right after *Honey Boo Boo*!

Steve clears his throat. Jessica looks like a Scandinavian Barbie, bored to tears. Finally, Declan stands and lets go of my hand, but plants a very territorial paw on my shoulder. He gestures with his other hand.

"Why don't you join us?" I swear he growls. Just a little.

Chuckles would be *so* cowed by the look I give Declan. In fact, I think I'm channeling my cat via astral projection, because I become pure evil via my eyes.

Declan just winks.

Winks! How can he wink when I am killing him with my laser death stare?

Steve rushes to sit down next to Declan, leaving Jessica to stand there, the right corner of her lip twitching. Or a bubble of Botox broke free. Hard to tell.

She clears her throat. Steve ignores her, about to open his mouth and say something to Declan. He looks like a golden retriever puppy who can barely control himself from pissing all over the foyer as he waits to be let out.

"Ahem," Jessica says again, looking at Steve with an icy glare that even he can't ignore.

Declan remains standing the entire time and gallantly walks over to her chair, pulls it out, and inclines his head. Her face cracks into chunks of ice the size of glaciers, and a smile that could act as a backup disco ball emerges from her head.

Steve is oblivious. It's his job to remain so. He's a player, a mover and shaker, a guy with one foot on the next rung of the ladder no matter where he's at—as he reminded me a million times while we were together—and he's got his eye on the prize, and the prize isn't Jessica any longer.

It's Declan.

Who looks at Steve like he wants to deworm him.

Meanwhile, my heart is dancing the cha-cha and my legs start to shake from nerves. Just then, the waiter comes to offer wine.

"We'd love to get another bottle of whatever Declan's ordered," Steve says in an arched tone, one he reserves for interacting with "the help" when we're in front of bigwigs. That makes Declan pause and look down at Steve, who is now sitting across from me with a look that says, *Don't blow this*.

Declan recites a few words of French to the waiter, who turns as if to go.

"One moment," I say. The waiter stops. "I would prefer a lighter white wine."

"You ordered the beef," Steve says, frowning. "Of course you drink red with beef." He knows I'm a steak girl, but the way he says it makes me bristle, a streak of self-loathing fury rising in a straight line up from belly to throat. The assumption that I'm a rube who can't possibly know what she's doing was part of the foundation of our entire relationship.

Worst of all? I reinforced it. Not the rube part, but the belief part.

Declan says something else in French to the waiter, who nods to me and walks away. Then he turns to Steve and says, "You know my name?"

Steve laughs in his fakey-sophisticated way. He doesn't seem to realize how obviously pretentious he is. I see it, Dad saw it from the first handshake he had with Steve, Amy sees it, but so many people Steve worked with never saw it.

It was my mom's job *not* to see it. All she saw when she looked at Steve was Harvard and Farmington and little MBA-fathered babies all lined up and cute in their matching Hanna Andersson pajamas while sleeping in their PoshTots nurseries.

Declan's tight jaw and cold eyes tell me he sees it quite clearly.

"Everyone who's paying attention in this town knows who the McCormicks are," Steve says blithely.

Wrong answer.

Jessica is sitting across from Declan and I'm across from Steve. Declan's hand slips under the table and he leans toward me, hot palm landing on my thigh. Although everything below my waist is obscured by the table, it's damn obvious what he's doing to anyone observing.

Steve's face turns a pale pink I don't recall ever seeing, and Jessica's eyes roll so hard she burns twenty calories with the motion.

"Paying attention is a good quality," Declan says, turning his eyes to me. He gives my thigh a squeeze. I put my hand on his and try to move it.

It is granite.

Something in me snaps and floods at the same time, desperation and attempts at maintaining an illusion of control all melting away with a rush of pleasure. Maybe it's the wine I guzzled. Maybe it's the feel of Declan's hand on my leg, half on the cloth of my skirt and half on my stockings. Yes, the split was that bad.

Bad never felt so good.

Steve is cataloging me now, his eyes done with resting on Declan, instead looking at me as if he'd underestimated the value of a discarded possession.

The waiter picks this exact moment to return, carrying a bottle of white and four glasses. He pours a small amount in a glass. Declan does the necessaries, sipping and nodding with approval. I receive a nice, healthy glass of white wine and then the waiter pours a twin glass for Declan.

He offers some to Jessica, who nods.

Steve declines.

After replacing the chilled bottle in its ice container in a stand that now sits at my left elbow, the waiter asks Jessica for her dinner order.

"I'll have a small field greens salad with vinegar and oil and the tilapia."

Declan makes a noise of amusement and I try not to laugh. Salad and fish. Boy, did he call it. The only way not to start giggling is to drink my wine, which I do. All of it. Like it's Gatorade. I decide right then and there to order the biggest dessert they have on the menu and eat it with gusto.

Because I *can*. And it won't have maple in it.

Steve's eyes bug out of his head while Jessica keeps her bored expression, Maybe it's a new Xanax-Botox combo. Perhaps they inject the Xanax directly under the skin, because whatever it takes to achieve a flat affect that is so utterly devoid of emotion can't be organic. It must be manmade. Someone patented *that*.

Except it all morphs when she talks to Declan. The ice queen becomes a sweet, warm princess and she is hot to snag him. Not that I have a claim on him or anything, though the way his hand is learning the terrain of my inner thigh makes me think he was a geography major with a keen interest in cartography.

I don't stop him. I don't want to. And he's showing no signs of wanting to, either, as his fingertips graze against my skin, moving in light circles, taking their time as they feel their way through questions I know the answers to now, but can't quite put into words.

Good luck, Jessica. You can't compete with Toilet Girl.

But you just keep on trying.

Steve alternates between looking like a ferocious business insider and a wounded intern. I can tell the landscape of his internal sense of the pecking order of the world has been deeply shaken. Accustomed to treating me like a social necessary at dinners like this, he used to think he had to carefully coach me. As if I were a walking liability ready to spring a *faux pas* at any minute and ruin his chances for success.

And yet I loved him. Still kind of do. Because even now, with Declan's hand practically typing out all the sexy scenes from *Fifty Shades of Grey* on my leg in morse code, a part of me wants to help Steve. Whatever that means.

"I saw the exhibit your brother has over at the Bromfield," Jessica tells Declan, taking the opportunity to reach out and touch his forearm. My eyes lock on her perfect, slender hand, and suddenly the only meat I want between my teeth are those fingers.

The possessiveness makes my body go on high alert, and Declan's hand stops moving. Even he can feel it. He shifts his arm just so, enough to make her drop her hand as he reaches for his wine glass, giving me a sidelong glance that tells me the message was most certainly received.

"The Bromfield is a gallery for modern art," Jessica says pointedly to me, leaning around Declan. She says it like she's a children's television show host explaining a new concept to an imagined four-year-old audience.

"I'm more a Fountain Street Studios kind of gal," I say as I reach for the bottle of wine in the bucket next to me. Steve's eyes widen a touch, the signal obvious. I'm supposed to wait for someone else to pour it, or to ask Declan or Steve to, or I'm supposed to disappear into a giant sinkhole created by the gravity of my lack of manners.

Instead, I pour the rest of the wine into mine and Declan's glasses, and gently return the bottle.

"Fountain Street?" Jessica says, eyes as wide as saucers, a sarcastic curl to her lip as she looks with fake helplessness between Steve and Declan. "I don't believe I've heard of them."

"They're in Framingham," I say, pretending not to notice the condescension. She sniffs, expecting the men to join in her game. Framingham is a former working-class town with a city center that is not even the kind of place where Jessica could imagine her cleaning lady would live.

"The old warehouse?" Declan says. "The one that the artists took over as a sort of co-op?" His eyes light up. "We've had commercial photographers from that operation come and do beautiful work for our promo materials in the real estate operation. High-end, quality work."

Jessica's eyes open wider, but this time driven by something other than coquettishness. A sharp look at Steve makes him literally sink a bit in his chair, as if his balls were deflating by the second.

"Have you been to one of their open houses?" I ask. The place advertises every few months, and I've always been curious.

"No, but I think we're about to. It's a date," he whispers, loud enough for Steve and Jessica to hear. She leans back with her lemon face again and Steve reaches for her hand with a loving look on his face. She tolerates his touch like she's getting a pap smear. Including the shudder, as if cold steel slides along her skin.

Declan and I reach for our glasses of wine at the exact same moment, and he hold his out to mine. "A toast!" He looks at Steve and Jessica, and they both pick up their wine glasses, Steve letting out a sigh, as if he'd been holding his breath for too long.

"What shall we toast to?" Steve asks.

Declan looks down in contemplation, and his hand opens on my leg, massaging up and down. I don't even try to pretend to ignore it now, loosened up by the wine and his attentions—both public and private. Doubts fade as the scenario sharpens. Crazy as it sounds, Declan's got his hot palm on my skin, his eyes on me, and his words, I suspect, are about to center around me, too.

"To...shopping for a billionaire!" Declan declares.

Chapter Eleven

Jessica inhales so sharply she sounds like she's having an asthma attack as she exhales. Steve greedily takes a sip or ten of his wine without clinking glasses with anyone.

Declan gently nudges my wine with a punctuated connection of glass on glass, and eyes that blaze with so many unspoken words. His hand that moves from my thigh, up over my hip, and to the small of my back speaks a few thousand of them, though.

"I thought you were going to say, 'To Toilet Girl,'" I confess quietly, leaning toward him. My lips are so close to his ear I could lick it. Only his slight movement backwards stops me, as he's out of reach with a shift of air that makes me want to breathe him in forever. He could bottle that scent. Pure Declan.

He chuckles softly. "Too easy. Besides," he murmurs, "if you really are on the hunt for a billionaire, you're batting zero with me. I'm not even close. But you're technically shopping for my father's company, and *he's* one."

Before I can answer, Steve interrupts, and in a loud, commanding voice says, "I can't compete. I'm only a millionaire." Fake self-deprecating chuckle. Jessica gives him a honey-cheeked smile, one I thought she reserved only for men like Declan, who are an order of magnitude beyond Steve. I know— and Steve knows—he isn't really a millionaire. "On paper," he used to say. Um, okay. Even I, a mere marketing major, know that if you have $1.5 million in assets you're not a millionaire if you also have $1.2 million in debts.

But what does a silly Mendon girl with a bachelor's from UMass know? I'm guessing Jessica is a Wellesley girl. Too fragile for Smith, and too moneyed for Wheelock. Then again, she has a graduate degree from Harvard.

Steve's gaze penetrates me, the look cold and hungry at the same time. As much as I hate it, he rattles me. It's been nearly a year since he dumped me, so while I'm not a raw pile of goo living on ice cream and espresso between healthy doses of self-loathing and a nice injection of desolation, he's still the man I thought I would marry. The guy who helped me have my first orgasm. The man who cheered me on at graduation. The one who patiently explained pivot tables on spreadsheets.

And *hello*? How rare is that? Because you can find anyone to have sex with you, but a pivot table expert who can explain it all in plain English? That's some rare stuff.

Declan feels exotic. Extreme. Like a crazy risk you can only grab at a handful of times in your life but that you regret not grabbing for. Steve was the dependable, rusty old lawnmower in the garage.

104

You weren't riding it anywhere special, but it would start up every spring just like you came to expect it to, and it would always be there.

Until it wasn't one day.

My analogies are getting really stupid as the wine makes me stretch with an unexpected yawn.

"Size doesn't matter, right, Shannon?" That's Jessica's voice, coming from left field. "Size of the bank account, I mean," she adds, winking at Declan.

Even Declan seems shocked. I think that comment would shut my mother up, and make Chuckles give her a high five. It's so…catty. That thump you just heard?

The sound of Steve being dumped.

I feel kind of bad for him, but it's hard to do that when Declan's thumb is stroking my soft skin with whisper-light brushes that make me move slightly, just enough to make a rush of molten lava pour through my veins, my body one big thrumming pulse of need for him.

Wait! This is a business meeting. I'm not supposed to be leaning against a wall of muscle in a bespoke suit, the scent of my own rose corsage from my prom date…er, business associate making me tingly and open. I'm supposed to feel bad for Steve as his entire conceptual framework for how the world works flushes away (see how I did that?) as the waiter delivers our food.

I see he ordered the filet, too. We used to find that endearing, and yes, I ordered white wine with my steak back then. Until he was in his final year of his MBA, he found that endearing, too.

Right now, Steve is so focused on Declan he doesn't seem to realize that Jessica just insulted his penis and bank account, and somehow managed to make me her girlfriend confidante. Impressive to do all that in one sentence. Perhaps I've misjudged her. If Chuckles were here, he'd defect to Jessicaland, happy to be united with his ancestral tribe.

Another glass of wine is needed to fully dissect the layers of Ms. Jessica. And a scalpel, too. Though she looks like she's been under more than enough scalpels, if you know what I mean.

We all—except for Jessica—pretend she didn't say what she said, instead *ooohing* and *aahhhing* over the food. I am feeling more and more like this is a date, and Declan confirms it by taking my hand and putting it on his thigh.

Oh, yes. I can *feel* how much this is a date, all right.

"How long have you two been dating?" Steve asks out of the blue. Holy *non sequitur*. The question is directed at Declan.

Only.

"We're not dating—"

"Since this morning." Our voices ring out in unison. You can guess who says what. Jessica gives her version of a snort, which sounds like a kitten sneezing.

I give Declan a distinct WTF look and Steve glances down into Declan's lap, obviously spotting my hand doing its own version of Magellan's circumnavigation of big, round objects.

No, it isn't that bad, but in dim lighting with an

overcharged tension between the four of us that could power a small town for a week, it doesn't look very businesslike.

Which means I just fulfilled Steve's prophecy about me.

I just don't know how to act properly in these sorts of settings.

Then again, he may be thinking that I'd never felt him up under the tablecloth of a fancy restaurant, surrounded by big-deal makers, but I have no idea whether that is true, because my phone starts to buzz.

My purse is right next to my thigh, so I leap into the air a bit, startled, my hand on Declan's lap whacking the underside of the table and ricocheting back into his lap so hard he makes a very uncomfortable *ooomph* sound that makes Jessica and Steve both arch their right eyebrows, like synchronized cynics. If they make that a sport, they'd win the gold.

"Sorry," I whisper as I simultaneously unzip my purse and stand. Bad move. Three (or is it four?) glasses of wine plus stiletto heels plus my ex-boyfriend and his date and an overly attentive business colleague so fine I could suck shots out of his belly button and have it called art by the Bromfield Gallery folks means the room spins and I crash back down into my seat.

Except it isn't my seat.

"Business meeting," Steve says as Declan snuggles with me in his lap, his nose nuzzling my neck, his arms wrapping around me less out of a lascivious nature and more to make sure I don't slide off and land on his feet.

"The best kind," Declan says, not looking at him. Jessica takes one bite of her fish and looks away.

Bzzzz. My phone won't stop buzzing. I stand again, more sure-footed, and excuse myself, walking away as fast as I can. Fortunately, the restaurant is fairly empty, and my lurching goes without notice.

The women's room is down a dark hallway with fake candles lighting the way. Monastery wine cellar look. It works. I get to the entrance in front of the ladies' room and look at my phone. Amanda, of course.

> *Did you get the account?* she asks.
> *And bring condoms?*
>
> *Yes and yes,* I text back.

What? Of course I brought condoms. Bought new ones, too, because it's been so long the ones I have might have reverted to their original element forms. I might not *plan* to have sex with Declan, but I'm damn sure going to plan just *in case* I have sex with Declan.

Kind of like buying a lottery ticket. You can't win if you don't play.

> *And...?* she writes.
>
> *Yes,* I text back, cryptic on purpose.

Make her freak out. Chuckles would be

pleased.

>*To which?* she types.

>*We got the account,* I explain. *The other one depends on Steve.*

>*STEVE? Are you still carrying a torch for that asshole? We need to get you exorcised,* Amanda types back.

It's so hard to read her. She keeps her emotions hidden so well.

>*Steve is here. At dinner.*

My phone rings suddenly. I answer it.

"Where are you and what the hell is Steve doing on your date with Declan?" she snaps.

"Business meeting," I insist.

"You bring condoms to every business meeting you have? When we get the dental association account, you seriously bring condoms for dinner meetings with Dr. Jorgensson?" Dr. Jorgensson is the current president of the association and is in his late eighties. He looks like a nicely dressed orc. He has a home health aide attend all our meetings.

"Yep," I say. "Even with him. Can never be too prepared."

"Why is Steve there? And speaking of people I would sleep with before I'd ever touch your ex, Dr. Jorgensson looks damn fine compared to him."

"Hey! I slept with Steve and that's really insulting."

Silence.

Then: "I'd still choose the colostomy bag over that piece of – "

My phone buzzes with a text. "Gotta go. But we got the account!" I say in an excited voice.

"That is awesome," she says, not ready to let me go. "But what is STEVE doing there?"

"He and his date"—*bzzzzz*—"appeared out of nowhere."

"Where are you?"

I tell her.

She emits a low whistle. "Your car's Blue Book isn't close to the bill Declan will have for dinner."

"I know."

"And Steve brought—who'd he bring?"

"Some chick named Jessica Coffin. Boston Barbie."

"Jessica Coffin?" Amanda says her name like I'm supposed to know who she is. "Oh my God. Steve is fishing in big waters."

"Well, she clearly thinks his fishie is little."

"What?"

"Never mind." *Bzzz.* "I really have to go."

"Call or text me later!" Amanda says.

"Tell Greg the good news!"

"And you have fun, too. Let loose. Be wild, Shannon. It's about time."

Click. I tap over to messages. It's Steve:

I think fate brought you here tonight.

Oh my God.

110

Chapter Twelve

And then he writes:

> *I've never seen you so vibrant. In command. You're perfectly poised and professional. I just want you to know I'm proud of you.*

Huh? This is the guy who spent two entire days of a conference berating me for using the wrong fork at dinner and now he's saying this?

Shannon? He texts immediately, as if the handful of seconds have been far too long for me to pause before replying like an eager dog catching a bone.

> I type back: *Nice to see you, too, Steve. Jessica seems like a great woman.*

Gag.

Another text, except this one is from an unknown number.

> *I have a cold spot on my thigh. It needs your hand to keep it warm.*

> I type back: *Sorry, honey! I'm at a*

> *business meeting. The kids need a*
> *bath and Johnny's homework needs*
> *to be signed. I'll be home late!* <3

And then texter's remorse kicks in, because it seemed funny when I wrote it, but now, as entire nanoseconds stretch into cavernous eternity, I eye the exit and wonder if I can actually walk that far with four glasses of wine (it's definitely four) and a heart that is attached to bungee cords that stretch two hundred yards with each adrenaline surge.

> *That's fine,* Declan texts back. *I like to role-play, too. How about you wrap yourself in Saran Wrap and I'll get a pound of chocolate-covered strawberries and we'll see what we can do with that after the kids are in bed?*

> *Dark or milk chocolate?* I text back, heart now attached to the back of Evel Knievel's motorcycle on a jump.

There's only one right answer.

Silence.

Silence.

Silence.

Both, he replies.

"Goal!" I hiss, like an Italian football announcer, only quiet.

"You okay, miss?" A waiter walks past me with a frown on his face, brow creased with concern.

I hold up my phone screen. "Just reacting to a business text. Clinched a deal I've been waiting to land for a long time."

He smiles and walks away.

I look down to find a new text from Steve:

Can we do dinner tomorrow night?
I'd like to catch up.

I don't want to answer that, so I lean against the thick, oak-paneled wall and take a deep breath.

"How long?" says a warm baritone attached to a (near) billionaire.

"How long what?" My frantic mind rushes off to erotic places all too quickly. Bad girl. Good, bad girl...

"How long have you been waiting to clinch a deal..." Declan repeats, closing the space between us through sheer will. I swear his body doesn't even move, but then it's there, warm and pulsing against mine. "...like this?"

His lips taste like grapes and hope, full and respectful, pressing against my own with a lush connection that makes me eager for more. Stepping in to the kiss, his body meets every inch of mine from thigh to shoulder, one hand sinking into my loose hair, capturing the back of my neck as if I am about to fall, his other hand around my waist, splayed against my hip.

Instinct makes my own arms wrap around his waist, sliding under the fine wool of his jacket to

113

find cotton as finely spun as silk, my fingers dancing on it as they ride up. His knee nudges my legs open as he pushes me into the wall, searching for every spot on our bodies that we could touch without being charged with a crime.

The feel of his cheek against mine, his hands everywhere, his groan mingling with my own gasps transports me. Nothing else matters. No one else exists. The insanity of the day, from how we met to our business meeting to this business dinner…

We are getting down to business, all right.

I break away and meet his eyes, wanting to see that this is real. *Real.* Not part of my imagination or something I read in a book and transposed onto my life. That Declan isn't kissing me out of pity, or a cheap booty call, or for any of the rare reasons men used on me as their own drive and baser natures made them view me as a tool.

No. What I see in his eyes reflects what I feel, and then I am the one kissing him, reveling in the starbursts of ignited recognition that something truly unique—life altering—thrives between us, nurtured only by this shared joining.

Our embrace is so strong, so tight, the slant of his mouth commanding and fiery, tongues communicating through touch in a way his fingers had earlier, but with more urgency and so much passion I think we might break the wall if we push any harder against it.

"Shannon," he murmurs, pulling away. The withdrawal of his mouth feels like a kind of mourning. He looks at my chest. "I crushed your corsage." That's not the only reason he looks at my chest.

I laugh, a throaty sound of delight, so genuine that my mind feels blank with a kind of clarity that seems unreal, even as it grounds me. I open my mouth and pure joy comes forth:

"You are the best prom date ever."

He dips his head down and our foreheads touch. His eyes turn to green triangles with his own genuine smile. We must look like complete idiots, and the idea that this is a business meeting went out the window a long time ago. Actually, I think that idea was flushed from the start.

"What made you kiss me?" he asks in a low voice that promises to make coffee and bring it to me in bed in the morning.

"You kissed me!" I answer, my hands on his shoulders now. I bat him lightly with one hand.

"Why?" he insists. I can tell he won't let me squirm out of this one. My phone is buzzing like mad and I imagine Steve is about to send a search party after us. Big deal. Who cares.

I look up, a few inches between us, and his eyes change. He's taller than me, arms protective and he wants me. *Wants*. Not just *desires* me, not just *likes* me. Wants. Craves. I am irresistible, and the part of me that finds that laughable is sitting back in wonder, thinking she got it *all* wrong for many, many years.

I close my eyes and sigh. "You had me at 'both.'"

* * *

Read what happens next in the *Shopping for a Billionaire* series in *Shopping for a Billionaire 2* at major eBook retailers everywhere!

Ready for More?

Sign up for my New Releases and Sales email list at my blog to get the latest scoop on new eBooks, freebies and more:

http://jkentauthor.blogspot.com/p/sign-up-for-my-new-releases-email-list.html

About the Author

Text JKentBooks to 77948 and get a text message on release dates!

New York Times and *USA Today* Bestselling Author Julia Kent turned to writing contemporary romance after deciding that life is too short not to have fun. She writes romantic comedy with an edge, and new adult books that push contemporary boundaries. From billionaires to BBWs to rock stars, Julia finds a sensual, goofy joy in every book she writes, but unlike Trevor from *Random Acts of Crazy*, she has never kissed a chicken.

She loves to hear from her readers by email at jkentauthor@gmail.com, on Twitter @jkentauthor, and on Facebook at
https://www.facebook.com/jkentauthor

Visit her blog at
http://jkentauthor.blogspot.com

Made in the USA
San Bernardino, CA
28 November 2014